THE FOURTH FLOOR

by

Peggy Hargis

The contents of this work, including, but not limited to, the accuracy of events, people, and places depicted; opinions expressed; permission to use previously published materials included; and any advice given or actions advocated are solely the responsibility of the author, who assumes all liability for said work and indemnifies the publisher against any claims stemming from publication of the work.

RoseDog Books
585 Alpha Drive
Suite 103
Pittsburgh, PA 15238
Visit our website at *www.rosedogbookstore.com*

ISBN: 979-8-88729-069-0
eISBN: 979-8-88729-569-5

CHAPTER ONE

Alex was up and ready to go to the office when Max called her since she was on her way to pick him up.

Hi Max. I am on my way out the door. I will see you in a bit. Is Madison there yet?

Yes she is here. I will see you when you arrive.

Alex hung up her phone and went out the door, down the steps and into her car. It was a hot day out and the weather reporter said it was supposed to rain this afternoon

At the office Max was already outside waiting on Alex, he opened the door and got in. They made their way to see the medical examiner.

So what do we know about the victim? Asked Alex.

Some kind of poison. The nurse thought that it was put through the IV. She was fine when the nurse checked on her last night and a couple of hours later the alarm went off in her room and when the nurse got there to check on her she was gone. So the head nurse thinks that someone had gone in after the nurses had changed shifts and did it. Usually at night once everyone is asleep they are on downtime but they are busy checking charts from that day, so no one really noticed anything going on. And her room was not visible from the nurse's station. It is too bad because she had knee surgery and was supposed to go home the next day. Max was sure it was someone outside of the facility that had gone in and done it. Maybe someone that was around the area and there are no cameras on that side, just at the main elevator.

So did they take the stairs or the Elevator? Alex was confused as to who could have done something like this because why would anyone want to kill someone that just had knee surgery? Unless someone had revenge on her? Maybe they were jealous? Ex-boyfriend? They had to get on this right away.

Well, whoever did it had gotten out without being seen because all of the cameras had been checked and they found nothing. They even checked for clues and did not find anything either. How can someone get in or out without being noticed? Max had figured that it must be someone who worked there before and knew the hospital well enough to sneak in and get out without being seen. And the victim must have done something for them to go out and kill them.

Alex pulled into the parking lot of the hospital and went in the back door. They knew their way around the hospital since they were used to going to the medical examiner's office as that is where most of their victims had gone. Jane had been on the job now for fifteen years and was very good at finding anything unusual about the cause of death to the victims. She did very good detail and checked everything on each victim so as to not leave anything behind. Other hospitals had tried to get her to work for them but she was dedicated to West Vale Hospital. Dr. Smith was over the staff and he ran the hospital with expertise. Only the best staff worked for them. He followed all the rules and went by the book on all employees as well as patients. Only a few nurses have been fired for not following protocol.

The hallway was empty and Alex and Max had gone to Jane's office. She was sitting at her desk working on paperwork. Max knocked on the door to let her know that they were there.

Jane looked up and saw that it was Max and Alex. She got up and handed them the paperwork of their latest victim. Here is all the information. Her family had already come down to claim the body. I have her in the lab. Let's go and look at it. There are a large number of rash patterns around her abdomen and on her legs. She had the largest lethal dose that is why she died so quickly. Whoever did it knew what they were doing. And they did it through her IV.

Jane got up and they walked down to the Morgue to look at the body. Jane pulled a drawer out where the body was. Her name is Dawn Brown. She was 34. Jane pulled the sheet down so that Max and Alex could see the body. See the rash spots?

Yes, that is a lot of them. Well, we are done looking.

Jane pulled the sheet back over and put the body back in.

The family is looking for answers and they think that it is the hospital that is at fault.

I can see how that looks for them. It happened here and someone should have seen something, replied Alex. Thanks for everything.

Ok, so I need a list of everyone that came into contact with her. Looks like according to the paperwork that she was given a dose big enough to kill two people.

It was done so that she would die quickly. Whoever did it wanted to make sure that she would not come out of it.

Ok well, we will gather up all the information and call us with that list.

I will get right on it, replied Jane.

Thank you so much, said Max.

We will go over to the station to see the officers who were at the scene of the crime when it happened.

Sure thing. I hope you find out who did it soon. I do not want this to happen again. They need to put up a better security system. I have told them that before but they will not listen. Said Jane.

So you knew that something like this could happen before?

Yes, something did almost happen but we caught the person in time before they were able to do anything. That person was arrested and is still locked up today?

Are you sure about that, asked Alex?

As far as I know, yes. It happened last year. There is no way that they would let him out already because he was found guilty of attempted murder replied Jane.

I am concerned that it could be someone that is working for them. Do you know the person that was convicted if they worked here before? Asked Max.

No, it was no one that was employed here. But they came in without being noticed and then were seen leaving after visiting hours. Replied Jane

Ok so it can not be the same person but am sure it is someone that knows the person and could be working with them. But why try to kill someone in a hospital? Asked Alex.

Because at night it is not as noticable. And it's not always someone that they know. Sometimes it is someone that has put out a hit on someone. It is an easy job and no mess to clean up. And if they do not have an IV to go through they will inject the person with the needle.

That is done all the time. And this is done without much notice. There was another hospital that had fifteen deaths before they realized how it was happening. They all happened within a six year span. After that all hospitals have been on alert. And now it is starting back up. I think that most people have forgotten what happened and this just seems like it is too easy to do. The adviser is going to hire more security, especially at night.

That would be the best idea right now. They may not hit again here but someplace else.

Our Fourth floor is our physical therapy floor for patients that need extra help and once they are well enough to go home with help. There are only a few nurses that are on that floor because they are needed more on the other floors. Jane was proud of their fourth floor staff and their efforts of getting patients back home with their families. Even though she does not work on the other floors she knows what goes on all the floors. That is how involved that she is at her work.

We will be in touch. And please give us a call if you suspect anything new or a possible suspect.

I am not here at night so I really do not know how I can help that way. I had only heard about the incident the next day. But I have more knowledge of the hospital than most here. I have worked on all of the floors, I did not just start out here at first. I started out on doing transport so I learned the layout of the hospital that way.

Do you mind giving us a tour. Just do not say that we are here for the latest murder. We do not want other people talking. How many people know about the woman found dead up there?

Just the night staff that was on that night but who knows who else because people like to talk. Most people are not able to keep something like this to themselves.

Right and news that spreads like fire. And usually by the time it hits the last person something in the relay of words has changed.

Well let me show you around. If anyone asks any questions just let me talk to them. We do not want people talking or asking more questions. The less we talk about what had happened that night. The less that they know the better and we do not need the patients knowing anything.

My mouth is zipped shut, replied Alex.

Good ok we will start on the fourth floor as it is the top floor. Let's go.

Up on the fourth floor everyone was busy with patients. There were only four nurses on the floor with ten patients. It usually is not as busy like the other floors because this is the area that the patients are in therapy. There is also a therapy room there that the patients go and do their therapy sessions at.

I am not going to say anything to anyone on the floor unless they talk to me first because I do not want to bring attention to ourselves.

They walked through the fourth floor and looked at the stairway. Anyone could come up through there without being noticed. Jane made notes as well as Max. He wanted to know how these people were getting in.

Let's go down the stairs on the way down. This way we can find out just how someone can get in and maybe hide until visiting hours are over.

That could be the bathrooms. And if they have on scrubs they can easily come in with them and not get noticed. Our scrubs are not of any color on the floor so our staff can wear what they want. But they have to have name tags on.

That is true. How many times do nurses lose their nametags?

Workers lose them all the time. Some are more responsible than others but they can fall off when working with patients so it could happen.

So it would not be unusual to find a name tag just laying on the floor somewhere. All they had to do was turn it around so that the name is not showing but it would definitely look like that they worked here. Max wrote that in his notes.

Yes it is possible. I sometimes find them in the bathroom laying on the sink while the nurses or aides wash their hands. We never had to worry about anything like this before.

Not once did an employee notice that they were walking around the unit. Many of the patients were in their rooms in bed, some had visitors sitting in chairs next to them talking about what was going on with their families.

Max and Alex followed Jane to the stairs, they looked at the door that was next to the stairs and saw that it was a janitorial room. Anyone could sneak in here?

I agreed, replied Jane. It is right by the stairs. I wonder why they made it like this when they built the hospital.

Max opened the door to the stairs and looked out. On the side of the wall he could see the water pipe which is easy to get to if there should be a leak. And that must mean that at each stairway there is a Janitorial closet.

Makes sense now replied Jane. And the room was on this back wall so all they had to do was go in the room and then make sure that the area was clear and then sneak into her room to give her the dose.

Let's go down on the third floor and see if they have the same set up.

They all went down the stairs to the third floor, Opening the door they immediately saw a door and opened it. It was a Janitor's closet. All of them had a floor sink for mop water.

It's much easier to clean the floors on a daily basis, sometimes even more and the staff is able to get to it if they need to clean up a spill. Jane was glad that she had found this out now that she has an idea on how the killer could have gotten onto the floor without being noticed.

OK well we will look into this and talk to the Sheriff's office to talk to the ones that were on the scene.

Ok and let me know what you find out. Jane turned and went back down stairs to her office.

Well we had better get going. We still have to go to the sheriff's office now that I believe that we have figured out how they were getting in. But they should probably be able to secure it better.

Yes but even still they can get off the elevator and say that they are checking on a patient and still get into their room.

True. Well anyways let's get to the next stop.

At the Sheriff's office Max and Alex went in and stopped at the front window. We are here to talk to the Sheriff that was at the hospital the other night for a murder investigation?

Oh yes that would be Sheriff Massey. He is out on a call right now but I will give him a message.

Max gave her a card and told her to give it to him and to please have him call the office.

Ok, I will do it. Thanks. I hope that they find who did it. That was just horrible. I know the aunt of the victim. The family is really taking it hard.

I am sure Alex replied.

Well let's go back to the office and see if there is anything new.

Sure. Do you want to order out and have food delivered?

Yes we can do that. Or we could go to the diner.

I am sure Madison would like to get out. I don't think that she will be too busy today. We really do not have much to go on yet.

At the office Max and Alex walked in and Madison was working on the new project. Well I just got a call from Jane, The lab found arsenic in the victim's body.

Oh well that is something new. I have never heard of anyone around here using that to kill someone. I did not think that there was access to it around here. Max took out his notepad and wrote that down in it.

Since when did you start carrying around a notepad?

Since this last murder. There is something different about this one. And I hope that it is the only one.

So Madison would you like to go to the diner for lunch today? asked Alex.

Sure I am starving. I did not get to eat breakfast and my snack bar did not last long.

Great, let's go.

At the diner they walked in and saw an empty table. Max waved at one of the waitresses and she came over with three menus

Your waitress will be right over. Can I get you something to drink?

Coffee's all around. We need our coffee today.

Sure thing. Coffee coming up.

Well let's not talk about the case right now because it needs to be kept out of the listening ear.

Fine with me replied Alex. Looking over the menu she was in the mood for the special. Chopped steak with mashed potato and gravy. Yum

Oh that does sound good, replied Max. I think I will have the same thing.

I am going to have a cheese burger with fries replied Madison.

The waitress came back over with the coffee. Well your waitress is on break so I will take your order. Is everyone ready?

Yes two orders of the Special and One cheese burger with fries.

Sure, do you want soup or salad?

Salad for me replied Alex.

I will have the same, Max said.

Soup for me replied Madison.

Sure I will put your order in.

Thanks, replied Max.

Just then Max's phone rang.

Hello, Yes this is Max. Oh hi. It was Sheriff Massey. Yes we can meet you later. Yes, that would be fine. See you there.

We are meeting him in two hours.

Oh good. Now hopefully we can see what he had found. Hopefully some kind of clue.

The food came out and everyone was quiet for about ten minutes.

So what are you going to do for the weekend? Asked Max.

Not really sure replied Alex. I know I have to do my usual cleaning on Saturday and getting groceries.

Oh yeah I need to get groceries this weekend. And laundry. I hate doing laundry. I think I am just going to relax this weekend. Still getting over the last trip we made.

Oh that's right how was it? Asked Madison.

It was wonderful, replied Alex. We had so much fun and even got to see the whales. It was so much fun. And such a needed trip.

Well I am glad that you had fun. It is always great when you can take a trip and get away for a bit. Even if it is a few days.

At the Sheriff's office Max and Alex went to talk to Sheriff Massey.

Hi my name is Max and this is Alex.

Hello, we can talk in my office where we can talk in private.

They followed him into his office and Sheriff Massey closed the door.

Have a seat.

Thanks for talking with us. What did you find, asked Max?

We found a pack of matches on the floor from a bar in Sugar Valley.

That is not far from here. So I am wondering if that is where our suspect lives.

Probably not. It's not likely that they live in the area but were visiting someone at the hospital. They knew the person that they killed somehow and had waited till they were asleep. It looks like it was done before visiting hours were over. Since the victim was already asleep the nurses just thought that she was asleep for the night. They had already given her the medicine at dinner time so they did not want to bother her when she was asleep. And she was in the room alone as her roommate had gone home that day.

So it was easier to get in and get out before anyone had noticed.

Oh ok. Anything else?

Yes they have children. He does not have custody as he had lost custody so they are with her family right now. They have been there since she went into the hospital. Her parents are very upset about this. Their last name is Watson.

Well thank you so much for all of this information. Now we have to find out where her parents are and where we can talk to them

I have their address. He handed Max a copy with their address on it. They have the children now. They are making the hardest decision right now as they have to go to court for custody for the children. The court knows that the father is not to get them at all. He has a claim against him for child endangerment. He was caught with drugs when they were in the house.

So he will never be able to get them back. That is good. Much better to have them there with the grandparents then to have them with a father that is not taking care of them right.

Exactly. Well I am sure you have work to do. I would definitely get over to the grandparents house today and talk to them. Ok thanks so much for all of your help today.

You're welcome. I hope that you can find this guy. Or we find him. Either way I want to see him behind bars.

Yes, me too. No money in the world is worth that much to kill someone. I mean why would you. It's not like you can go far if you have family. Someone is going to turn them in I hope.

Alex could not believe that someone would kill someone that they do not even know. Most of the murders are from those that know the person. It is just sad that people think that they have to have someone that they once loved or was supposed to love that murder is the only way. Or that they hate that person so much that they feel that by killing them is a way to get back at them. Here he lost his kids so he may have taken it out on her by having her killed. If he is not able to have his kids then she would not either. Whatever happened to divorce. The other spouse usually finds a way to get revenge.

It happens all the time. I see it on the news more than what I really want to see. But it is usually the husband killing the wife or the other way around. Some people are very possessive. If they are not able to have the person anymore then they do not want anyone else to have them either. But I think that most of it is just because they feel betrayed so they get back at them in a not so good way. Max had a friend that killed his wife and now he is in prison for life. All because she had moved on and found someone else.

It is so sad. I know it is hard to try to move on when you love someone that much but it would seem that they would do everything to make the marriage work even more.

Not always replied Max. One person can have an obsession for someone and when that marriage does not last then the obsession becomes a danger. Even if the couple do not get married it can become dangerous for anyone. Love is not one sided.

Exactly understand that. Love is hard to figure out sometimes. People fall out of love. Or they love someone and then find out that they are not who they are at all. Maybe it would be good just to stay single and just have friends.

Oh you can't be like that. We have someone out there, we just have to find them that is all. We can't be afraid to love someone. We just have to be careful who we let love us.

Max was right, Alex thought. But she was in love with him. She had never told him or even hinted that she was having much feelings for him. She could never let him know that because she did not want to ruin their friendship.

So what is that address on the paper we can go by and see if they are at home. I know that they want to find out who killed their daughter. So sad that the children have to grow up without their parents. Sure the father is still alive but he has no chance now to see the kids.

Alex looked at the address, ok so it's down on Marcal street. That is a few streets up from here.

Ok that is good. Not far from our office either.

The road is right up here. Take a left at the light. The house number is 230.

Max turned onto the road and they found the house and there was a car in the driveway. Two children were playing outside.

Max pulled up in front of the house and got out.

A man stood up and called the kids inside.

Can I help you? Asked the man. It was the victim's father, Mr Watson.

I am sorry to bother you, said Max. I know that you have a lot going on right now but I hope that you can answer a few questions? My name is Detective Max Lee and this is Detective Alex Tibbles.

Sure I can answer some questions. Not sure if I know the answer to all of them but I will do my best. My wife is not up to answering any as she has taken our daughter's death really hard. You know she was supposed to come back here until she was able to be on her own with the kids and now she is gone.

Do you know anyone that would want to hurt your daughter? Ex-husband or Ex-boyfriend?

Her Ex-Husband was abusive to her and the kids, more verbally then hitting them. He did not start out like this until he got into drinking and the drugs. I told her to leave him but she claimed that she loved him. He went for help but then he would go back to his old ways again.

I am sorry to hear that, replied Max. Can you tell me anything else?

Well he had threatened her when she took custody of the children. He did not like it that he had no rights to even see his kids. She got full custody. She got child support but only when he had a job. He quit more jobs than he actually had all together. After he was not able to see the children he just got worse, more into drugs, then into meth sales, he was locked up for awhile after that. He had gone mad. He did not even look like himself anymore. He looks more like an old man. That is what drugs do to you.

Well I am sorry that she went through all of that.

So what are you going to do about the Ex Husband?

We are going to talk to him as well. And to see if he has a record.

Oh he does. For assault and battery on an ex-girlfriend before he married our daughter. He claimed that he had changed. Then there was talk that he has been doing this sort of thing since before he got out of highschool. You need to put that abusive man in prison.

We will definitely look into that. We will follow up with you on any details that we find out.

Well I have to go. We have to finish up the funeral arrangements for her. To bury a child is so much harder than losing a parent. We are supposed to go before our kids, not the other way around.

I understand, replied Alex. Her cousin had lost a baby at birth. Such a sad thing to go through for any parent.

Max and Alex turned to leave and to go back to the office.

Well I believe we found our killer. It has to be the husband, said Alex. I mean who else could it be. Anyone that was abused like that I am sure would not want to have a boyfriend. I know I wouldn't.

I agree, said Max. It would turn anyone away from a relationship after that. It is so hard to find the right person sometimes.

I totally get that, replied Alex.

Well by the time we get back to the office it will be time to go home. We can call it a day. I wonder if Madison had left already. We will have to put this information in the new file for Madison to go over and work on the information collected already.

At the office Madison was still there. Hello, replied Madison. Someone called about the Detective job. He is from Georgia and just moved here. He has been a detective for five years. He left his number. His name is Bill Johnson.

Ok thanks,replied Max. I will give him a call now. We can use all the help we can get in this case. We really need to get a car out to watch the Watson House. Just to be sure that the children are safe. If it was the husband he may come and collect his kids.

So we can call the police department and have them watch the house for the night. Said Alex. I can give them a call now.

Sure that would be a great idea. Just in case. If he knows that his kids are at the grandparents he might try to get them back and run with them. Max went into his office to call Bill about coming into the office tomorrow to talk.

Alex went in and called the police station and told them the situation for the Watsons. They sent an undercover cop out in an unmarked car to sit out for the night shift. Thank you so much, replied Alex. It would be greatly appreciated for their safety.

I agree, replied Clay Martin. He was the police Sergeant. We do this sort of thing once in a while and I will put out my best cop to do the job. I will have someone there tonight. I just need the address. Alex gave him the address and hung up the phone.

Alex and Max left the office for the day and stopped out to the diner for dinner. They talked about the new case.

Well I think it must have been someone else, Alex said. I am not sure that the husband would be able to do it without getting noticed.

Do you think so? Maybe if he does seem to be unstable. But who would he get to go in and kill her?

Someone that he trusts. Maybe a family member or close friend. But we have to find out who would be willing to do something like this to Dawn. We need to find out more about her and what she did for a living.

We need to talk to her parents for more information.

The waitress came over and took their order and left.

You know it seems funny now that she goes in to have surgery and is about to go home and is now killed. Why not find another way to do it? Asked Alex.

The parents must have a key to the house if they have her belongings from the hospital. I will have to call them said Max. And they needed to go there soon before someone had started to go through the things at the house.

The waitress brought out their order and the drinks and then left.

Oh this looks good, said Alex looking at her spaghetti.

Yes it does said Max actually now wishing that he had ordered it himself but cut into his steak. The baked potato was still hot with the butter melting inside and dripping down the side.But I am actually glad that I got this. Everything looks so good. Even the green beans.

Would you like a little bit of my spaghetti? asked Alex.

No, I am fine. Just enjoy your dinner. I am glad that we did this. I did not know what I was going to have for dinner so this is perfect. No dishes to wash after.

Right. Living alone I usually have a hard time finding things that I want to eat. Sometimes I like to get the meal packs and then I have left overs for another day.

Oh I have done that too, replied Max. I actually like to do that more than doing a single meal because then I do not have to worry about dinner for the next day.

So this weekend I have to deep clean my living room and bathroom.

Oh that sounds like fun.

Not really but it needs to be done. My bathroom has not had a good cleaning in a long time and it really needs to be done.

Do you need any help? asked Max.

While Alex would love to have Max come over and help she knew that she would not get anything done. No, I really need to get it done on my own. I like to listen to music while I clean.

Ok well I offered, said Max. Guess I will just sit around at home all alone and be bored.

Ok well maybe Sunday but we will see. I might have you over for dinner.

Sounds like a plan, replied Max.

Alex made it back to her house and checked the mail. Nothing but bills, She opened the door and put the mail on her desk. She was tired as it had been a long day for her. She went over and turned on the TV and watched the news. Nothing much on tonight for the news. The weather for the next few days was going to be cooler. Alex was not ready for cooler weather, she loved the summer months. There is just so much more to do in the summer. Although if she were able to travel farther than just two hours away it would be even better. She wanted to go to Florida for the winter for Christmas. Hopefully this year she will get to go. Now that they have a new person maybe joining the team she would be able to get away then.

CHAPTER TWO

Alex walked into the office and found Max and another man talking. It must be the other detective talking about the job. They did need another person to help work the cases. Or at least to take a case if needed.

Oh you must be Bill Johnson? Said Alex.

Yes I am. I moved up from Atlanta Georgia. We had a great team but I just wanted to move somewhere different.

Well we definitely could use you on our team. We get several cases a month and we could use the extra help.

Great. I would love to join you both. I have been able to solve even cold cases. I stick with them until I find out who did it.

We do have a few that we had to close. Maybe sometime you can look at them and see what you can find to open the case back up. We just had no other leads but I would really like to get them solved.

Max went into his office and pulled out one of the files and handed it to Bill. You can pick one of the other rooms as your office. One has two desks in it for two people to work in. It is the same size as mine. The other is more private with one desk if you like your privacy. I am currently looking for a few more people to work with us.

Ok thanks Max replied Bill. I will look this over and see what I can dig up on it.

That would be great, said Max. Some fresh Eyes is always helpful. Our receptionist should be here soon. Her name is Madison. We will break for lunch around noon. Right now we need to work on our case and gather up more information.

Bill went into the larger room and sat down at the desk. There was a phone and a printer at his desk but he would have to be supplied with a new computer.

Oh I will pick up a computer now for the desk and a few other things as well and download the program so we have access to files for victims.

Madison had just walked in the door when Max was about to leave. Oh Hi Madison. Look, I am going to go to the store and pick up a few things for the office. I should have done that earlier but did not plan on expanding until later in the year but we really need to get more people hired to look at these other cases. I will be back later. Our new detective Bill is in the big office.

Sure that is fine. Anything new on the case you're working on?

Nothing yet. Hopefully within the next few days we will have more information.

Ok well I will see you when you get back. I am glad that you have found someone else to help out with the other cases.

Max came back with the new computer, a more expensive desktop that will perform better than a laptop for what kind of work that they do on a daily basis and is more secure with the new virus blocker on it. He brought it into Bill's office. It has all of the latest technology on it and it has the new virus protection on it so that no one can hack into the files when you're working on them. I also picked up a laptop if you need to work from home to work on the cases.

That is awesome. Yes, thanks. We had a computer hacked into and the person was arrested.

Max went to Alex's office, anything new to report?

Well the officer on duty last night outside of the Watsons Residence said that he had spotted a car parked down the road with someone sitting in it for over an hour until they finally decided to leave. He thinks that it might have been the father.

Ok well it is a good thing that we have someone out watching the house. We need to set up cameras out back to monitor to make sure that no one is able to get in. We have to make sure that they are not able to get to the family and do harm.

What about moving them to a safe house, asked Alex. Or even put them up in a hotel?

If we do that then someone might report back to the father that they have been moved and they will not come back to the house again. What we need to do is get a van and set it up with surveillance equipment and hopefully catch who is watching the house. If they see that we are there they won't stick around. But if they suspect that no one is watching anymore then they will come back and try something.

That is true. So we need a van with no windows and maybe a black curtain to shut out any light that might be on in the back so that someone can sit in the back and watch the cameras and then when they see activity of someone getting into the house they can move in on them.

I will stop by the police station to see if they have a vehicle that will work like that. Maybe have it look like a commercial work truck that way no one will suspect anything. It will look like that someone lives in the area that works for the company.

Great idea, said Alex. I know that the family will be glad when this is all over.

Yes and I will too. Then we can all sleep better. I think it is time for lunch and then we can go over to the station to see what they have for surveillance equipment.

Bill, would you like to go to lunch with us? Asked Max.

Sure I am ready. Then I can get back to work on this case. I had heard of this case before and I feel so bad for the family. I watched it on the news.

Yes and I hope that we can get it to rest.

Alex had stopped by Madison and asked her to lunch.

No. I am going to eat my salad that I have and stay here and try to work on what has been processed so far.

Ok well we are going to the diner and then to the station to see what we can get set up for the night time watch.

Sure thing said Madison. Good luck at the police station.

Thanks, replied Alex.

At the diner they all went in and sat down at an empty booth. Well get what you want. I am buying lunch today. Tomorrow Alex is buying. Max smiled at her.

I can do that. Welcome to the team Bill. I hope you like working with us.

I like it so far. The area is great and my new apartment is nice too. The people here are really friendly.

Oh nice, where do you live, asked Max.

Holly Heights out on the Boulevard. It's brand new so the apartments are beautiful.

I heard of them, replied Alex. They do sound nice and not that expensive.

Does it have a pool? Asked Max.

No but it does have a membership discount for the tenants at the gym in the city.

Are you joining?

I am thinking about it. I like to work out. I also run five miles in the morning.

Impressive, replied Alex.

Well what is everyone going to order? asked Max.

The fish looks good. Have you tried it yet, asked Bill.

It is very good, replied Max. I usually get a vegetable to go with it instead of fries.

That would be a good choice since the fish is already fried. I try to eat healthy.

They have broiled too, said Alex. That is really good.

Oh maybe I will get that instead.

The waitress came over and got their order and said hi to the newest member of the office.

This is Bill. He is working with us now.

Well hello, said the Waitress. My name is Tina. Then she turned and walked away.

Wow she never talked to us like that. She must like you, Alex said.

That is nice. But I am not looking right now. I had a bad breakup before moving here.

Oh that's too bad, replied Alex. I had trust issues for a while myself for the longest time. My highschool sweetheart had met someone else in college. So I had just decided to put everything that I had into my work here. I had liked it like that but now not really. I am gradually getting into trusting people again.

Well that is good. It will be a while for me. She took everything from the house that we had lived in. I was gone for a week on an assignment and when I came back my house was empty. She had moved someplace else and had movers come in and clean the house out except for my stuff.

Did you not want to go after her for the furniture?

No, it's not worth it so I moved here and got all new stuff in my apartment. I love it there.

Glad you like it.

The waitress came back out with their food. Here you go, enjoy.

Thank you, said Alex. We always do.

Glad to hear that, said the Waitress. We love having you come here to eat.

After lunch they went to the police station to see if they had a van with no windows in it that they could use for the stake out. Just to see what is going on, they can also use some cameras inside as well to keep observation on the house.

Great idea, said Bill. I will be glad to do the stake out at night. While you keep things going at the office.

I will try to pair you up with the undercover cop so you have a partner out there. We will have to get a camera inside the home. Just so that we are able to see for sure what is going on.

They walked into the front office to see if Clay Martin was in.

The girl at the desk recognised them when they came in. Are you here to see Clay?

Yes we are.

I will see if he is here. He was out on a call earlier.

Ok thanks, replied Max.

You're welcome.

The girl at the desk calls Clay's office. He picks up. Hi there are three detectives to see you. Two of them were here the other day.

Ah yes, send them back please.

Sure.

The girl at the desk hung up the phone. I can buzz you through. When you hear the buzz just pull the door open.

Thanks, Max. Have a great day.

You do as well.

Max heard the buzz and pulled the door open. They walked in and found Clay's office and knocked on the door.

Clay came to the door and opened it. Hello, come on in.

Hi replied Max, we have a few questions to ask you since you have been set up with surveillance at the house but I wanted to get some more just in case they got into the house.

Yes we have all that equipment.

Good what about a Van? With no windows asked Max?

Yes we use a white one for that kind of job. We also have a black one but we usually use the white one since it is more common to have for work trucks.

Ok great. Are we able to have Bill here work with your undercover cop at night?

Yes, that would be fine. I would rather have two men on the job and back up close by just in case. But only if they see something going on. I think that they will try something soon because they will try to grab the kids as soon as they can. So we have to be ready before they do. And I am sure that they are going to try to harm the grandparents to get to the kids.

That is what I was wondering too, said Alex. That would be horrible. We can't let that happen.

We are also going to go to the calling hours and funeral tomorrow as well because we have to be sure that the father does not show up. Or anyone that will try to grab the kids. The father may not show up but he might send someone there instead. So we have to be there just in case.

I agree, replied Clay. I have seen this happen many times where the kids are there and not long after they are kidnapped by their other living parent. So everyone has to be treated as a possible suspect at the funeral. I will have a few more cops going as well.

Thank you so much, replied Max. I do not think that we will have to wait very long. I think someone will try something soon. Ok well tonight we can set up for the van. We can get the inside of the home hooked up and the van to sit outside this evening.

Bill if you would like you can go home and get some rest so that you can sit out tonight. I think that they will try at night time more than the day because they won't be seen as much at night time as they will during the day.

Yeah that would be great as I want to be awake and alert tonight. Coffee for tonight to keep me awake.

Ok well we will do the services tomorrow so you can rest for tomorrow night.

Thank you, replied Bill.

Well planned out, said Clay. I like that. We will have a cooler in the van for drinks and water.

Back at the office Bill got into his car and left while Max and Alex went in and started to work on their plan for tomorrow. Tonight should go well.

I really do not think that anything will happen tonight but it will happen after the funeral. I do not think that he will try anything at the funeral.

I agree, said Alex. We really have to be on the watch after that. Especially if they have family coming to the home after the funeral for food. I know that some do that or they might even do it at the church. Everyone just brings something to eat after the funeral and talk. It is sad that more people do not get together much anymore with family and they happen to gather at the funerals. I still do not know all of my family because they are spread out all over the States.

Well most of mine are still in South Korea, said Max. But all over South Korea. Seoul is nice but it is expensive to live there. The smaller apartments are reasonable though and they are very nice for one or two people. Seoul is very nice there and many celebrities live there in secure areas but they cost way more than I could ever afford.

Well I would love to come with you one day and visit and see where you had lived and where you grew up. That would be really nice.

It is beautiful there. I will be happy to show you around.

Thank you Max. I just have to save for the trip. Now let's get to work on what to do next.

Well we have to plan on what we are going to do at the services. We have to be able to watch the family and keep close eyes on them, especially the children. We have to watch the family to make sure that they are not going to try anything either. The grandparents would not think that family would be up to something but they just might be.

Well we better get over to the grandparents home to talk to them now but let me call them to make sure that they are at home.

Max went into his office and filled out more paperwork while Alex called the Grandparents and they were at home. Max put the paperwork aside to finish after they got back because this visit had to be early enough to go over everything that was going on at the home. The children had to be included so that they could be aware that someone might try to come after them.

I will drive, said Alex. You drive all the time, let me drive this time.

Ok that's fine. I trust your driving. Besides we have gone on two trips already and you have not wrecked us yet.

Well I am always a careful driver, smiled Alex. I would never do that to us. We have a very important job to do. Just do not get on my bad side and you're safe.

What? You mean you would do harm to me if I do? I better rethink it the next time you ask me to go somewhere with you on a trip.

Oh don't worry it will happen when you least expect it. Alex looked at him in a threatening way and then smiled.

Well I better be on alert then. As it can be at any time. I have to sleep with one eye open.

At the Watson's house they knocked on the door. They could hear the children playing in the house.

Mr. Watson answered the door. Surprised that they were back he said hello.

Can we come in? asked Alex. We would like to talk to you about the night watch.

Sure, said Mr. Watson. Come on into the kitchen. Would you like some coffee?

Not for me, said Alex.

I am ok too, said Max. He pulled out a chair and sat down at the table. Why we are here is that we have two men that are watching the house at night. The police station has an officer driving by during the day to do a check. If someone is to come and get the children they will come at night. We would like to put up a camera inside the house so that the guys outside can make sure that you're all safe.

We saw the ex-husband out in his car yesterday again. He just sat there staring at the house and then finally left. I kept the children inside and I closed the curtains in the home so that he could not see in.

Good idea but we do not want them to know that they are being watched. So just go about your day like normal. We are hoping that they or he will come here or at the funeral and try to slip in unnoticed. We really think that he will send someone to get them instead so we have to watch everyone. We will set up a camera out back and one out front, the one out back will be able to monitor the back and the one side of the home and the front will be monitoring the front and the other side of the home. They will be put in a tree so they are not easy to be seen from the road or the house.

Where is Mrs. Watson now as she needs to know about what is being done. The children need to know that their father or someone might try to come and get them.

We do not let them outside without one of us. I am usually the one that goes out with them. She is not strong enough if someone tries anything. She has health problems. I take care of her and the kids. But we were talking about moving out west with the kids so that he would not be able to find us. I am sure that he did it or had it done.

What is his name? We never got his name.

It is Carl James Brown but CJ for short. I warned her about him. But she said that he would change and he had changed but then went back to the way he was before.

Ok thank you. I appreciate any information that you give us to help us with finding out who did this to her. Do you know of anyone else that would want to hurt her?

No not at all because she kept to herself after the divorice. She spent a lot of time here on the weekends. The kids have a room upstairs because they come here in the summers while their mom works. I will go and get my wife and the children.

Thank you. And we can also make the school aware not to let the children go with anyone except you and your wife. Because they might come to the school and try to pick up the kids. As long as the school is aware of what is going on.

Mr Watson went into the living room where the children were watching TV and called them all out to the kitchen. This is my wife Mary.

Hi Mary. Nice to meet you. We are here to discuss what will be taking place at night. We will have a white van parked out front just a few houses down from yours but they will be able to see the yard and inside to make sure that you're safe. If they try to break in we will know it and we will call for backup to come and arrest him or them.

Do you mean that Daddy is going to come and get us, asked Sam?

Well maybe Alex said. He may try to. But your grandparents have temporary custody of you.

We want to go and live with Daddy said Sarah.

Dawn's two children only knew their father when he was not drinking and doing drugs, only when he was sober until he went over the edge again. They did not see the real side of their father. Dawn never let them see how their father really was. She raised her children to be independent and that drugs and alcohol were no good.

Why do you want to go and live with your father? Asked Mr Watson?

Because he is our daddy, Sarah replied. I miss my daddy. Why can't he come and live with us here?

Well because he has been into trouble and he needs help, replied Mr. Watson. Your grandmother and I want you to live with us so we can take care of you and to raise you right. You are much better off here with us.

But why asked Sarah? Why does daddy need help? What is wrong with him? Is he sick?

Yes Sarah he is sick. And he needs help but he has to do it himself. No one can make him get help.

Has your father tried to pick you up from School Sam?

No but I did see him sitting in the parking lot once last week. It was before Momma died

You never told us, Sam said Mr Watson.

Well I did not want you to be mad at him. That is why I did not say anything and then I forgot about it. Sam started to tear up. I miss Mom. She has been gone for a while now. When is she going to come home?

Well Sam. Like I said before, your mom is now an angel. She is in heaven now and she is not going to come back home. I know it's hard for you to understand but she is gone.

Oh. Ok. Well Come on Sarah lets go and watch Cartoons. A tear ran down his face as they both walked back into the living room.

Awww that is so sad to see him cry. They both must be going through a really rough time without their mom.

Yeah they both are taking it really hard. They miss their mother. It is hard for children who live with their mom. They have not been with their dad for sometime.

Well we do not want to keep you too long. I know that you need to process all of this. And I wish you good luck at everything and that you're able to get full custody of the children.

Thank you. We hope to be able to do that. If not then maybe her cousin who was close to Dawn, they were like sisters.

Ok well we will see you tomorrow.

Ok and Thank you for all that you are doing for us.

Back at the office Max and Alex went into Max's office to talk more about the case and what they were to do tomorrow.

The service is at ten in the morning and will last until noon for visitors, then the funeral is after and burial after. Someone needs to be with them. Max started to fill out the paperwork again and finished them. I am going to give Madison the paperwork for her to work on tomorrow and file it in the database and then file the paperwork into the file. We have to make sure that the kids are safe and that he is never allowed to get near them again.

Well are we about done for the day, Alex had some things to get done for tomorrow.

Yes we are. I need to go home.

Meet you here at nine tomorrow. We need to be there early for the services.

I will be ready and waiting, replied Max. Who is driving?

I will pick you up. I will pick up two small coffees.

Ok see you tomorrow. I just have to finish up a few things and then I am going.

I will see you then. Alex turned and left, Madison was just getting ready to go for the day as well. Bye Madison. See you tomorrow.

Yes I will see you tomorrow. I will come in early at nine to be here when you both come in.

Ok I will see you in the morning. It would be good that way you can get a hold of us in case something happens while we are out.

Alex left, went home and got her outfit for the next day which consists of Black pants, White shirt and Black Blazer. That way if anything happens to where the father shows up she can move faster than she could with a dress.

Alex went to the kitchen and grabbed out a frozen dinner and put it into the microwave. She was not that hungry only because this case has gotten to her. She has never had anything like it. And it is sad that the children are the ones that are suffering the most here without either parent. Well hopefully it will be a closed case soon enough.

CHAPTER THREE

Alex got to the office and Max was standing outside waiting. Alex walked into the front door and picked up the paperwork to follow up on if there were any added notes to put down on it.

Good morning, You look nice this morning.

Thank you Max. So do you. We look like we are just two normal people that are there for the funeral and not looking for a possible suspect.

I just hope that everything goes well without any problems. The family does not need anything bad to happen today. They have gone through so much already. Max had on a black suit and looked so good.

Alex did not want to go to the funeral now but knew that she had to go and take him there. Boy did Max look hot. Alex knew that she would have to behave herself but darn it was going to be so hard. Ok back to the funeral.

Inside there were only a few people there including the grandparents and the children. Max and Alex went up to talk to them to let them know that they were there. They were going to take a seat in the back so that they could watch when people came in. To keep an eye on what is going on.

Thank you for coming, said Mr Watson. And for looking out for us.

Your welcome replied Max. Again so sorry for your loss. She looks beautiful today.

Thank you, yes they did a great job with her. The children are in the nursery with my sister, said Mr. Watson.

Oh ok. So we will keep checking there as well to make sure that the children are safe.

There is a baby monitor there so we can hear if anything happens. The children were just overwhelmed right now with the casket open. It will be closed during the service just for the children so that they will not be so upset.

Max and Alex went back to the back of the church and sat down. This way one of them can go and check on the children without being noticed too much.

The Church was getting filled with family and friends. Alex made it a point to sit at the end of the pew so that she could get out easily. Most had already gone through the line of the family and said their condolences and then went and sat down for the funeral. The service was not to start for another hour.

Mrs. Watson had gone to sit down as she was starting to look very tired. Mr Watson sat down next to her for a bit before getting up to stand again.

All of this must be very tiring for both of them right now. Said Alex.

Yes I believe so, especially Mrs. Watson. You can tell she is worried about the children, replied Max.

Alex had checked on the children a half hour ago and they were busy playing in the nursery. She knew that she should check on them again. She got up and walked out in the hallway and walked down to the nursery. The Aunt was sitting in a chair and the children were sitting at a little table listening to her read to them. Smiling Alex walked back to the sanctuary where everyone was at.

Everything ok asked Max.

Yes they are sitting listening to a story. They are so cute. So sad that they have to go through this at such a young age. They do not understand. Alex was sad because she had lost her grandmother who she was close to as a young girl. She used to go there and stay for the weekends. They would bake and make quilts. Watching her Grandmother bake pies were her best memories. Apple was her favorite.

Well I am glad that they are content right now, said Max. It gives them a break from reality right now. I am going to check around outside. I know that we have someone watching the entrance but I just want to make sure.

Ok, I will keep checking there too.

Max got up and excused himself by going through people talking together. In the hallway there were people there talking together as well. Max had overheard someone say that it was the husband that had killed her. He was positive that it was him and that he had heard him say it once that he would kill her to get the children back. No woman would ever take away his kids and get away with it, the man said. Max stopped and said, not cutting in but I was also wondering the same thing if it could have been the husband.

Yes well what man would let an unfit mother take the children from a man who could provide for them.

Why was she unfit?

She worked all the time. She had a career and her career was more important to her than the kids.

How do you know that Max asked? Could it be that she wanted better for her children? She had a good job not really sure what she did but she worked to provide.

To him she was unfit but I knew that she provided for her kids. Much better than what he was doing. Always out drinking and who knows what else. I had seen him flirting with the women there that go with any guy that they meet.

So not only with him drinking was he also having sex with these women? Asked Max.

Well I really do not have proof of that but knowing CJ I believe that anything is possible.

Hmmm ok well thanks. It's just a bad situation right now for everyone. Thanks for the chat.

And you are? asked the man.

I am Max, I am a friend of the family.

Oh ok. Nice to meet you.

Same said Max.

Max then walked outside and found several men standing around talking and smoking. Some were even hanging around a car with a man sitting inside. They happened to be parked next to his car. He walked around to the back of the car and popped open the trunk and acted like he was looking for something. He could hear them talking about the kids. He could not make out what was being said. Max had texted Alex to go and watch the children. While he was out there he found out that the man in the car was the father. The father was asking where the children were. He heard one of them say that they were in the nursery. So he had people there to find out where the kids were so that he could go and grab them. Max grabbed something out of the back of the car and closed it and then walked back inside. He went to the nursery and told the Aunt to take the children to the bathroom and lock the door.

He then stood on the side where he could not be seen and waited for the father to come for them. Fifteen minutes later a man came in and looked around and saw Max, he was startled and walked back out of the room. Max went after him. What are you looking for?

My child was supposed to be here. There was a woman looking after the children here and I came to get her to take her home. Where did they go?

I really do not know. They were not here when I came in. Max knew better that there were only two children in the room and he was not the man in the car. He was someone else that was coming in to check on the situation. The man left and Max watched him as he left the building. Max called for backup as the father was still in the car in the parking lot. Max had given them the description of the car and to have him picked up and brought back to the station.

Alex came out from the services and found Max looking out a window. Where are the children?

They are locked in the bathroom. Go tell them to go back to the grandparents.

Alex went back and found the Aunt and the children. It's ok to come out now. They are gone. Go back to the sanctuary. I will walk back with you.

The Aunt opened the door and peeked out and saw Alex. Ok well we got scared when the man told us to get into the bathroom and lock the door. I did not know why he had said that only to think that the father must be here.

Yes he was. So it is best to go back where you're safe with family and friends.

Max and Alex stayed with the family until the funeral was over and then went to the burial after. No one else showed up after. Max figured that the father would try to get them at a later date when this all blows over. To when he thought that it would be safe for him to come out. But he does not know that he could face charges for attempted kidnapping and possible murder charges. Max had managed to video the conversation for the Sheriff as evidence. That is the best thing about being a Detective on how to find ways to record a conversation without being noticed.

After the services everyone went back to the church for a get together dinner for family and friends. Max and Alex stayed for that and waited until the grandparents had decided to go home with the children. He knew that a team would be sitting outside just in case. If they can prove that the husband had killed his wife or had her killed. Either way he can go away for life if he is proved to be guilty. But they still had to find more evidence.

Max and Alex went back to the Office. There were no calls or anyone stopping in so it was a quiet day for Madison. Max went in and made a report in the case file about the incident that happened today. Alex I still think that it was the husband that did it and he had planned on doing something with the kids. It's just not right. If you get a divorce things should not be as difficult for those that just are not able to accept. But then again I have not been married and have no children so I really am not able to say. What ever happened to getting a divorce, go your separate ways and support the kids like you normally would?

I really do not know. I had a friend who is divorced, the kids go to their fathers on the weekends and they do well together. Not everyone can live with other people. Some people are just meant to live alone and they prefer it that way. Said Alex.

I agree. I have an Uncle that was like that. He never married. He was engaged a few times but they never worked out so he decided to just live alone. He was happy that way. He got to do what he wanted and he traveled wherever he wanted to go. Max paused for a minute, then said but you know what, he passed away and no one knew it till his sister went to check on him one day and found him sitting in his chair dead. He was there for a week. I could not go to the funeral at that time. He was a great guy. He had all kinds of stories about his trips. He loved life. Up until he was eighty-nine. We tried to get him to go into a nursing home but he fought us all on that.

Ah, I am sorry. That had to be hard for her to find him like that. And to die alone without anyone finding you until a week or so later.

Yes she had nightmares after that she said. Just something that you do not want to find. She had thought that he must have gone somewhere but where. He was not able to drive anymore at that time. And he was not in his right mind when he was there so he probably was not eating right.

I could not think about how that must have been to know that he was like that and then trying to get him into the nursing home and then to find that it was too late. Alex had never experienced anything like that and she hoped that she would not have to with a family member. It is hard enough with someone you really do not know.

I know and I hope I never have to do that either with any of my family or friends. The memory would just stay there.

Well I am going to go for the day, Said Alex. Do you need me for anything else?

No you can go. See you in the morning. I need to find out what the guys have to report from tonight when I come in tomorrow. Hopefully Bill will have his report filled out.

I hope that the father will give up and leave the kids alone. When they are old enough they will be able to see him on their own.

Yes but they might not want to when they get older and find out that their mom was killed and that he might be behind the whole thing.

That is true. Well see you tomorrow.

Bye Alex. Have a great night.

You to Max. Bye Madison. See you tomorrow.

Alex got home and got her mail, there was a letter from her parents. Oh a letter. I love reading letters. Alex's mom usually sends pictures of them around Florida. She opened up the envelope and she took out the letter and read it, then looked at the pictures. They were her parents on the cruise. Alex could see that they had fun there. She then turned on the TV and turned on the news. There was a new store opening. Oh I think I need to go and check that out. It was a little toy store. She could go and buy the Brown Children some toys. I can go tomorrow and pick up a few things and bring them to the house. She figured it was the right thing to do.

CHAPTER FOUR

Alex pulled up in front of the office and went inside. Bill was talking to Max about the night watch. They found a car sitting in front of the house. Bill did not see anyone get out of the car. Bill could only tell that the driver was on the phone and talking to someone and then he drove off. No other incident for the rest of the night.

Well I am going to go home and get some sleep before I have to be back at the van for our night watch. How long do you think that we need to do this for?

Maybe up to a week. Just to make sure that the family is safe. We will keep the cameras up so the police station can monitor the house from there but until now we need to stay close just in case.

I agree. Well I am going to stop and get breakfast before going home and then I am going to sleep. I am so tired.

Ok, replied Max.

So Max, There is a new toy store that I want to check out and pick up some toys for Sam and Sarah.

What a great idea. We can go after lunch said Max. He cared about those kids and knew that they had a rough road ahead of them being without either parent has to be hard. Especially when they are their age.

Well lets go over what Bill's report has to say and file it in the folder.

Sure. Anything new asked Alex.

No, not really. Just a random guy sitting out front but across the street talking on their cell phone. Either they were checking in and giving info or they were just talking on the phone and had nothing to do with what was going on.

Well hopefully it was just someone calling someone or they got the call and just happened to pull over there to talk. But still it is always best that we keep tabs on the family for now.

Yes for sure. We also should go to the hospital to ask questions. There should be something that the nurses had seen on the other shifts. Max was sure that someone must know something.

I hope so. So that we can see if she had any visitors at all. I am sure that her parents had gone up to see her. Anyways I have a few calls to make. I want to find out what is going on with the father.

Ok sure. I will be in here working on the report and to see what our next step is after the hospital.

It was lunch time and Alex and Max had decided to go to the diner again. It was their favorite spot to go to as they had a large range of choices of food. So what are you doing this weekend? Alex had asked Max.

Cleaning. I have to get the apartment ready for cooler weather. The temperature is dropping next week. It won't take long though but I definitely want to get things done. What are you doing this weekend? Asked Max.

Basically the same thing I do every weekend. Catch up on laundry, get some Christmas shopping done early. I like to stay ahead of it. I am glad that I have the guest bedroom. I put all the gifts in there so I can get them wrapped and then I put them away in there. I wrap as I go. That way I do not have to wrap in December.

Great way to do it and get it done. So what are you going to get to eat?

I think I am going to go with the soup and salad combo. That really looks good.

I am going to go with the Reuben sandwich. Maybe a soup to go with it. Iced tea for my drink. Get what you want I will buy this time. Max was happy as he did not have much for bills since he lives in an apartment. Everything is included except for Cable and phone. He also has car payment as well as insurance.

The waitress came over to take their drink order and then left.

So hanging around the house all day is in your plans. If you want company on Sunday give me a call in case you get lonely.

Alex knew that he was hinting to come over in hopes that she would cook for him. I will see, she said. Will probably make a nice dinner on Sunday but I have to get groceries tomorrow so I will figure something out.

As long as it is not liver I am fine, smiled Max.

Oh well that is what I was thinking of cooking. Liver and onions. My parents used to cook it for me when I was a kid. I liked it but I never made it since I moved out. They would even invite me over sometimes for dinner and I would go. It's one of those dinners that you like once in a while but not all the time.

Whew, I thought you were serious there for a minute. I was going to change my plans quickly.

Oh you know I would never cook you liver for dinner.

I know you wouldn't. What do you want me to bring?

A bottle of wine. A red wine.

Ok deal. I can do that.

Well I am thinking of doing a roast so Red wine would be great with it.

Oh a roast with those little potatoes that you put in it and carrots. Yum and don't forget the onion.

I won't. I love those little pearl onions in it. And they do not take long to cook.

The waitress came over with the drinks and took their order.

Sorry about that, we had to make some fresh tea. No charge. So what can I get for you to eat?

I am going to do the soup and salad with Ranch dressing on the side, said Alex.

Ok and what would you like to have?

I am going to do the soup and a Rueben.

Great choice for both. I love their Ruebens.

Waitress turned and left to put the order in.

Well that is cool we got a free drink today. Max smiled at Alex.

Ok so why are you smiling at me now?

What? A guy cant smile at a lady without getting accused of something? Asked Max.

Maybe it just depends on what his intentions are, replied Alex.

Well I have no intentions. Just trying to be nice. Where is this toy store that you want to go to? Is it far from here?

It is out near the mall. I think it is across from it.

Oh ok. Yeah I think I passed by there the other day.

I do not think that they have many of their own toys as I don't think that the grandparents have gone to get the kids things yet.

That will be a sad process. To figure out what to keep and what not to keep and then to get rid of all of her belongings.

Yeah I know. It is hard to lose someone and then have to clean out the house or apartment after. But at least they will not have to buy the clothes

The waitress brought out the food. Enjoy your lunch.

Oh we will. We love coming here because the food and prices are great.

That is great to know. I see you come in here a lot. We have our morning crowd that comes in on a daily basis even if they come just for coffee. When we do not see someone that comes in daily we worry. But they usually come in the next day.

I understand that. They become family.

Yes they do.

Well now let's eat. We have some shopping to do. I also have to find something for my niece. She requested something else after I had gotten her things done already.

After lunch Max and Alex went to the new toy store. There were a lot of people there checking it out on their first day of opening.

What about a train for Sam? And a doll or stuffed animal for Sarah? Asked Max.

Train would be nice for Sam but I think that Sarah would much rather have a stuffed animal. I just feel that she would get comfort from it.

Ok well let's go see what we can find.

In the boys section they found a cute train set that was easy to set up and play with. It was made of wood so it would stay together better.

In another area they had seen all kinds of dolls, Barbies and stuffed animals. Alex picked out a cute kitten that was the cutest and knew that Sarah would love it.

Well now I have to find this one toy for my niece. It is an electronic game that she wants. She wants to play with her friends. She has a phone that she plays with her friends on as well but she likes this other game. I think it is made by Nintendo.

Oh yeah those have been around for a long time.

Yes they have. I had the first one that came out. It was a lot of fun. Anyways I think that they are over here where it says games. Alex and Max walked over and found the games, there were board games, card games and then there are the electronic games. Here it is. Alex was glad that she found it, There were only two left. They must be popular.

I guess so. Wow. Well, are we done?

Yes we got everything. Let's get this over to the Watsons.

At the Watsons Max and Alex knocked on the door. Mrs Watson answered the door this time. Oh hi. I am surprised to see you here.

We only stopped by to see the kids and to give them a couple of toys. I thought that they would like these.

Mrs Watson called out for Sam and Sarah to come out into the living room, they were playing in the bedroom that they shared.

Oh boy are these for us? Asked Sam.

Yes we got you a train to play with. And this is for you Sarah as she handed her the little kitty.

Sarah reached for it and took it then ran back into the bedroom. She came back out with a small brush. Now I can brush its fur. Thank you.

What do you tell them for bringing you such nice gifts?

Thank you, Sam and Sarah.

What are you going to name your kitten? asked Alex?

I am going to call her Bella.

What a great name Alex said.

Sarah smiled and sat down to play with her new kitten.

She just loves stuffed animals, said Mrs. Watson.

I think all little girls do. Replied Max.

Well we do not want to keep you, we just wanted to drop these off and we need to get back to the office.

Ok well thank you for stopping by with the gifts.

You're welcome. If you need anything please give us a call.

I will. Thank you again.

Alex and Max went back to the office to do their reports on the Watson Case. They were both sure that CJ had something to do with the murder of his ex wife. Killing her with an injection of Arsenic was ideal for him. Easy to do since she was not near the nurses station and no one really could see the suspect go in and give her the injection. What a perfect way to kill someone though Alex.

Well we have to hope that he opens his mouth and that there is a confession in the jail that he is in until he can be arraigned. Hopefully he will blab to someone that he trusts. We need an afformant to go in and check him out.

Yes, great idea, replied Alex. But who? We already have Bill on assignment already. We will have to see who is in the jail that I know and go in and talk to them. See if they know anything about the new inmate.

I know someone who is. He is there for vehicular homicide. I told him to stop drinking but he did not listen. Then one night he decided to go out drinking and had too many. Got in his car to come home, he just lived down the road from the bar, and hit a pedestrian on the way home. The victim's family is making sure that he does not get out for a very long time. So he has to pay the price but he was warned because I know what kind of person that he is when drinking. He is doing his time at the jail until they move him to the prison in another state. He is moving out towards Arkansas. He still has to go for his final hearing. So I will go in and talk to him to see if he has heard anything.

Wow I am surprised that he is not in prison yet.

Yeah here we have different standards for different things. And he was just arrested a few weeks ago. He regrets it every day. Like I told him, sorry does not bring her back. Max looked down on the floor, I knew her when she was a child. She was walking home from work that night.

I am so sorry Max. Why did you say something?

Because I found out just yesterday after we got done working. I think that he would be glad to help me with this. I am going to call the jail now and see if I can make arrangements soon to get this started.

Yes it would probably be better if you want to talk to him instead of the both of us.

He is allowed only one visitor at a time. Max then walked into his office to make the phone call.

Alex went into her office and brought up any information about CJ Brown. She did find him on social media and found his picture and it was definitely his profile. He was talking about Dawn and how he hated her and that she took his kids away from him. One post said that she will pay for what she had done. Alex had printed off the information for evidence. She knew that he had a motive but who had killed her. Alex went through his friends list. There was someone that she had recognized from the funeral. It was Tom Brown. Must be CJ's brother. Alex then looked up Tom Brown to see if he had an account. Bingo he did.

Max came into Alex's office, I will be back. The sheriff is letting me come in now to talk to Samual about CJ. To see if he can be our ears while he is in there. I told them that I need him in there a little longer to not move him to the prison yet. So I will be back later and make my report.

Ok well I had found CJ's social media page as well as his brothers so I will be looking around to see what else I can find and print off.

Great idea, I knew that there was a reason why I kept you around, he smiled. See you later. Hold the fort down.

I will. Madison is here to do that I have work to do. I will get the information I need and print it off for the judge.

Ok well see you later. He had his notepad and pen tucked in his pocket to write down any information that he needed for this case.

Alex went back to doing her research and found someone else that might be of interest. A Tom Jones. He is CJ's best friend and he has Dawn on his friends list. But why did Dawn keep him on her social media friends list? Why not block him. She would have to find him and see what kind of person that he is. What his relationship was with her and why they are still connected. Alex had noticed that he works at Lakeland Country club. He is a bartender there. He has many female followers so he must be a Ladies Man.

Max checked in at the Sheriff's office to talk to his friend Samual Jenkins. The girl at the window had contacted the officer in charge of the inmates and told him that Samual had a visitor.` He was then buzzed into the hallway to go to the visiting area to meet up with Sam, that is what he called him for short. He went in and waited for Sam to be brought in. After five minutes he was escorted in.

Well hello. How are they treating you here? asked Max

Better than I had expected, replied Sam. The food here is actually good. And the inmates are pretty good because they are not here long. Soon they will be released. I am the only one that will be sentenced to Prison.

Have you met a new inmate named CJ Brown?

Yes he said that he was accused and arrested under false pretenses. Why?

He is being held for possible murder of his wife.

What? But he seems so nice and is crying to everyone that he is innocent. He is trying to get people to feel sorry for him. But I do not as I really do not know him that well. Well we never know a wolf hiding under sheep's clothing. So what do you want from me and what is in it for me?

I want you to keep an ear out for talk to see if he actually brags about doing it or who he had killed his ex wife. And I will see what kind of deal I can get for you as far as prison term.

You do not need to get me a lesser sentence. Just some things that you can do for me on the outside.

Like what? Asked Max.

I need a few things. From my home. Like personal things. And then can you give my key to my mom so that she can get my things out of the house since it looks like I am going to be here for a while.

Yeah I can do that. No problem.

I am so sorry that this happened. I was too drunk to know that I should not have been driving from where I was at. I should have just walked home. I should have just left my car at home but I had gone to pick up a few things and then just stopped at the bar after. Now I have to pay for what I did and I understand that.

Well it is too late for that. I should have done this or I should have done that. I had told you to not go out drinking. I have seen too many accidents out there. It is too late for a lecture so I am just going to stop myself here. But thank you for doing what you are going to do for me. It wont make up for what happened but at least we can try to put the right person behind bars.

Back at the office Alex had already gotten everything that she could find about the other guys and the stuff printed off that she needed to hold in court. There are several posts that should actually put CJ in jail for a long time.

Hello there Alex. How is the search going?

Great. I think I may have enough to put CJ behind bars and whoever else that needs to be there. What did you find out?

Well I talked to Samual and he said that he could find out what is being said there. He is sure that someone will say something. He is a likable person there and many people talk to him anyway so he should be able to find out something.

Awesome news. I am going to file this away after you look at it for the night. She handed it all to Max for him to look at. It was getting late and she was ready to go home. Madison had left right before Max got back.

Max read all of the information and had handed it back to Alex. Very good. I think we got him. Tomorrow we need to check in at the hospital to see what the staff had to say if they had seen anyone. We have to find out as much information as we can. Max's phone rang. It was a number he did not recognize. He went into his office and took the call.

Alex had gotten everything put away just as Max had come into her office.

We have another body. Let's go.

Ok but where?

At the hospital. Guess which floor?

Oh no not the same one?

Yes.

A patient? Asked Alex.

No, a staff member.

Oh wow. So we know it is not CJ. So it has to be someone that he knows. He is contacting them from the Jail.

Yes, let's go.

At the hospital Max and Alex get on the elevator and push for the fourth floor. They get off and go to the nurses station. The staff is standing around in disbelief. One nurse is crying.

We are Detective Lee and Detective Tibbles. Can you tell us what happened?

Well we were here at the desk when one of the nurses came running over here and told us to call Security. She found our head Nurse in the supply room.

What is her name? asked Max.

Sally Moore. She was a great worker and was here all the time. She was great with the patients.

Max and Alex went to the supply room to look at the body. Sally was laying on the floor. She had been strangled with a wire. It happened quickly.

Why had they not used the same method that they used to kill Dawn if it is the same person. And why Sally? Asked Alex.

It would have taken longer and she may have gotten out of the room or someone would have found her before she died. The staff said that she was on her delivery of meds for a half hour, Only a few of the patients got their meds for the afternoon. One of the staff members had gone in for clean sheets and found Sally laying on the floor. She thought maybe she had passed out until she checked her pulse and found out that she did not have one.

Sally has worked here for several years. She had made friends easily. Why would someone want to hurt her?

Maybe she saw something that she shouldn't have. Max had wondered why someone would have anything against her as she was the head nurse. Did anyone have a grudge against her here?

Not that I know of, replied Jane. What about you Millie?

Nothing that I can think of. She was great with all of us. She helped us when she was not busy. Millie turned and walked away.

Everyone here is in complete shock. Why? Everyone is asking that question. Now that this is the second death within a week on this floor they are all scared. How did this happen twice?

I know it's hard and we need to get security up here now all the time. Max knew that they had to step up their game because not only was it Dawn but now Sally. Why are people getting killed and why only the fourth Floor? He knew that he had to talk to the owner to get more security on all the floors, not only the Fourth. Jane, we need to get a board meeting no later than tomorrow. Can we get one for today? I would rather have someone on this now.

I can get the leader to come in. Let me go down and call them.

Ok thank you, replied Max. I am not sure how long this will take Alex. Why don't we tell Jane we will be up in the cafeteria. This way we can get something to eat before we meet up with everyone tonight or hopefully in the morning.

Max went to talk to the staff on the floor. We are going to try to get someone up here to watch the floor with you, security. We have to get this taken care of now.

Thank you, we really appreciate it. None of us want to be on this floor anymore. I think it would be better if we moved everyone off and just went down to other floors. And for the other patients that are here for physical therapy to see if we can schedule someone to come into their home and do physical therapy with them.

Well for now I want everyone to pair up and stay together. This means no one is allowed to go alone to any room or anywhere.

We are short staffed now .One of our workers had called in and quit. She was just having a hard time with her anxiety when Dawn was found dead.

Well see if you can get some help up here from other floors. I would recommend on every floor that everyone is paired up together.

Ok well we can do this today but not sure how we are going to do it tomorrow. I am off tomorrow and now our nurse is no longer with us. The hospital will have to assign one for her now.

Ok well I am hoping that we can get this situated as soon as possible. And maybe if we can move everyone that is on that back wall of rooms, Are you able to move them together more out this way?

Yes we can do that today. We only have five patients back there.

Ok that would be better. We just have to block off that one section.

Max and Alex went down to Jane's office and told her that they were going to be in the cafeteria and that she could find them there.

Ok well I had just called the main board member and they are going to call a meeting for tonight to go over your thoughts.

Thank you, said Max.

After the meeting Max and Alex had left.

Back at the office Max had driven back to drop Alex off so she could get her car.

See you in the morning. I will definitely need coffee by then.

Me too. It's been a long day.

Alex got into her car and drove straight home. She was happy to be home to be able to shower and relax. It was still too early to go to sleep but she wanted to go in her bed and settle down, find a good movie before falling asleep. Her phone buzzed, Alex received a message. It was from Max saying Good night. She texted him back and put it on the charger for the night. She was happy that Max had told her Good night.

CHAPTER FIVE

Alex grabbed three cups of coffee and drove to the office. When she got there she saw that she was the first one there. She opened the door and walked into her office. She did some more research on Tom Brown and Tomas Jones. She found out that they both have criminal records. Well I am not surprised she said to herself. Tom Brown was arrested for burglary and petty larceny at a store. Tomas Jones has a record for Assault and Battery. Alex then went back to social media to look up their pages to see what they were writing on their pages as well as who was responding. Alex noticed that there was a Jack Naples that had commented on Tom Brown's post about hunting. Jack had written a comment, I have something for you to hunt. PM me later when you have the chance. Alex really wanted to find out what he wanted. Checking his profile Alex learned that he was married but his wife had left him. She wondered if the hunted was going to be his wife.

Max had walked in with Bill in tow. So you saw nothing last night.

Not a thing. Things may have blown over for now since the father is in jail. Once he gets out I think that is when we need to be back there to keep watch of the house. Since he is in jail there is no way he can have his kids.

You're probably right, replied Max. At least I hope you're right. But he could hide away the children with family until he gets out. Let's just wait until we get this case closed before we do anything else different because he still might have someone try to take the kids. Once we let our guard down that is when he will make his move. I am sure he has someone watching the house.

Yeah I agree. Ok we will keep watch outside the house. No one has really paid much attention to our van. We drive it there every evening and then leave in the morning so that people will not suspect anything. Well I am going to go home and get a shower. Hopefully I can get a good nap before working tonight. The neighbor's dog kept barking yesterday so I did not get much sleep. So I drank enough coffee yesterday to keep me awake.

Max walked into Alex's office to see what she was working on. Madison had not gotten in yet and the phone rang. Max had gone to answer it. It was Mr. Watson.

Hello Mr. Watson, how are you?

I have been better. Someone tried to break into our home last night, said Mr. Watson.

What do you mean they tried to break in? Someone has been watching this whole time.

Well they tried to get in through the back window. The screen was taken out. Thankfully the windows are all locked. We do not even open them anymore and wont until this guy is picked up. I have not said anything to Mrs. Watson because she doesn't like being here as it is right now.

I understand, said Max. I will have our men check the camera out back and maybe have them add one more for more protection.

Thank you, it is greatly appreciated, replied Mr. Watson. I put the screen back on while she was getting the children up and dressed.

You're welcome. We are on this.

Thank you again.

Max then walked back into Alex's office. So what do you have so far? I see you were working on something.

Well you know how people put out too much information on social media. I found someone that had commented on Tom's post. She showed Max the post and Jack's comment. Then she brought up Jack's page. She found his wife. Her name is JoAnna. Well we will have to check out her profile. We have to find her before Tom does and maybe kill her. I wish I knew what the message had said.

We would have to get Tom's computer to find out. If we can see what was sent when he is not there then we can find out what was sent to him. Find out what is going on. Or to get a warrant to see what he has on it. But we would rather go in and check without him knowing that we know. We will have to do it when he is home so one of us can distract him and the other one can look on his computer to find out what the email said.

Great idea. Well we will make plans for that hopefully this week. But we have to find the wife and maybe warn her and put her into protective custody.

We could go today if we can see if he is home. But this Jack guy has been married to his wife for ten years. I will look at her profile now. Alex brought up her Profile. She has two children in her profile picture, she works at the local drug store. Alex knew that Carl's Pharmacy was a busy one as she goes there herself. Alex knows the pharmacist. I will call and see if she is working today. We have to find out where she lives and then put her and her children up somewhere far away.

There is that place about two hours from here. We have to get ahead of this now before Jack realizes what is going on.

Hello I am here, said Madison. I had car trouble so I had to call a cab from the garage.

Hi Madison, said Alex. Glad you're here. What happened to your car?

I am not sure, it started to sputter and then just died. Thankfully I was able to get it pulled off the road. I have roadside service so that saves me on the towing.

Well I am glad that you're here now. Listen the hospital is going to be on tight security all over on all the floors due to the two deaths that had happened. I want to make sure that there are no other deaths happening at the hospital. The staff there is scared and they do not want to go to work until the person responsible is arrested. And quite frankly I do not blame them for feeling that way.

Max went to the office to get the file and brought it back out to Madison. I need you to type up a report of what we have so far. Then leave it on my desk. Bill's report is in there as well.

Ok, right on it said Madison. I hope we find the person or persons soon and get them behind bars. Now do you want to order in for lunch or are you both going to go out?

I think we will go out and you're welcome to join Madison. You are a great part of our team. I am glad that I hired you. Max had smiled at her and turned and walked to his office.

Madison sat down at her desk and got started on her report. She had a copy saved to send to the judge when everything was all done.

Alex was still searching on the internet for more listings for the men that she had discovered. CJ Brown had a few other profiles on Social media. She looked them all over and found out that he had another girlfriend on a site called The Cloud. I wonder what she thinks of him now she thought. After all, he was just arrested and sitting in jail. Alex looked up the girlfriend and decided to go and make a house call. She got up to tell Max that she had to go and run an errand and then left.

Amy Martin lives in a small house out on Sherman Ave. There was a car in the driveway and Alex pulled up out front parking on the street. She got out of the car and walked up the driveway and up onto the porch. She knocked on the door. She could hear talking in the background and then a woman opened the door. Hello, can I help you?

Are you Amy? Asked Alex.

Yes I am, why?

A man showed up behind Amy. Is everything ok? What's going on?

I will take care of it, just go and finish up breakfast.

Amy, do you know that CJ is in jail?

Yes I do. And what does that have to do with me?

Because we believe that he is behind the death of his wife and he may do the same to you. I just wanted to warn you so that you can prepare yourself until we can get him in prison. But I also want you to know that his brother Tom Brown, Thomas Jones and Jack Naples are suspects. Who is here at the house with you?

That is Dan. A friend of mine. Well CJ called me and wanted me to get ahold of his lawyer. I said I would. He said that he loved me and that he did not do it. I believe him though because he is not like that. He would never hurt anyone.

Honey, are you ready to come and finish your breakfast? It is getting cold.

I will be there in a minute, shouted Amy.

Well I just wanted to let you know because I think that you need to go somewhere until this is all over. I have a feeling that he will try to come after you. Two women are dead now and both at the hospital.

Who was the second person? All I knew was Dawn.

It was the head nurse. I am not sure why she was a victim but she was found dead. I can not go into any more details.

Oh I am sorry for both women. But I think I can go to a family's home to stay. Look I know that CJ would never do it but Tom or Tomas they both have a record.

So does CJ. There is a lot that you do not know about him that I found out. But I am not able to go into details. You need to be protected and go there today.

Ok I will. And I know that this looks bad with Dan here and everything but it really is not what it looks like. He has been my best friend since we were in grade school and I called him to let him know about CJ. Dan warned me about him and I did not want to listen. But I just want this to all be over. I still love CJ but I can not accept him if he had something to do with Dawn's death.

Ok well like I said get out of the house today. Do not answer your phone or tell anyone where you're going. You will be risking your life as well as the ones that you're staying with. Here is my card, call me if you need me or if you hear of anything.

I will, said Amy and thank you.

Alex got back to the office and she went into her office to make her report and to go over it with Max.

Wait, what did you just do? You went to talk to her without me? What if something had happened and I was not there to help you? Do you realize what you have done?

Nothing happened and I am fine. She is going to go to a family member's home to stay until this is all over.

So what did you find out? Asked Max.

She knew that CJ was arrested and in jail, he called her. She also had a male friend at her house. His name is Dan. She says that they are friends but he called her Honey. They have been friends for a long time. Anyways I told her about the nurse that was killed and that she might be next if anything happens. Once this is over and the rightful killer or killers are in prison. She is free to do whatever she wants to do. I just wonder what kind of guy this is that she is with. I did not get a last name. But I am sure I can find him on her social media page.

Well let's go head to lunch. I am hungry and Madison has been busy working and needs a break too.

You can't wait till I look online to see what I find on Amy's profile to see who this Dan is?

Yes I guess I can. I have some crackers in my office. But make it quick.

Ok, Alex went back to work in her office and looked up Amy on the internet. She found out that Dan was on her friends list. Alex looked to see just what kind of person Dan was. He looked clean. She found out that his last name is Sanders. Alex then looked up any arrests that Dan has had and found nothing. So hopefully he is not one of the suspects.

Max came into Alex's office, ok are you ready now? It's either we go or I am about to chew off my arm and eat that.

Well we would not want that to happen now do we. Or you could have just left and I could have met you there. Where do you want to go to eat?

I don't really care. I did not eat breakfast this morning. After last night I did not get up in time to eat anything and I was not hungry then anyways.

Ok well what about that restaurant that is an all you can eat buffet.

Sounds great, let's go.

Madison got up and went out with them while Max locked up and jumped in Alex's car. Madison figured that she would sit in the back and let Max sit up front with Alex.

Well you will love it there Madison said Alex. I have eaten there a few times and the food is great. They have all kinds of food there, anything that you want. And the price is also great.

Oh good thanks Alex. Great idea.

At the restaurant it was busy, but it held a lot of people. It was lunchtime and people were leaving so that was also good. They walked in and got in line, got their drink and paid for the Buffet. The inside smelled so good of all the different types of foods.

My stomach is growling, replied Max. Can you hear it?

Alex listened for a bit, Yes I can. She laughed.

They got to the cashier and Alex paid for everyone to eat lunch. Then they were taken to their table.

Ok I am on my way to get the food. See you later. I may leave you a crumb of food in the pans.

Oh so you're going to leave us with no food? But why? I mean I know you're hungry but you better leave us food.

Well we won't see him for a bit. He is gone. He must have worked up an appetite.

Most men do. I do not know where they put it and still look thin. Madison laughed. My late husband was like that. Until he got sick.

Oh I am sorry. So are you all alone now?

Yes. I like it that way. I miss my husband but I do not want to be with anyone else. I am too old for the dating scene. I like to come home and only have to look after myself. It does get lonely sometimes but I am fine with it after. I go out and get something to eat, usually I pick up dinner and then bring it home. I like to watch Netflix. I can come and go when I want. I do not have to answer to no one and I can go on trips alone if I want. I usually like to travel places. I did not do much of that this year because I had just moved into the area and I am still unpacking my place.

I understand. I live alone as well. I get lonely. I live out with no one really around. It is really quiet there.

Oh nice. My place is small but just big enough for me. I moved from a two story home. We had five acres on it.

That is nice. I have three acres on mine. My parents lived there but they moved to Florida. My parents went on a cruise.

Oh nice. Well we better get in line for food before Max eats them out of business. He does like to eat. You know he is still a growing man.

Yes, I like him. He is a nice man and so good at what he does. You do as well. You're both very nice to me and you hardly even know me. Thank you for asking me to come today.

Hey what are you both still standing around gabbing for. Go get your food and come back and talk. Otherwise we will be here all day.

Well I guess you will have to walk back to the office since I drove.

Ouch. That hurt. But I am fine with walking. Max smiled and sat down to eat his lunch.

Ok well I hope you left us some food. It looks like you got everything off of the buffet.

Yes I almost did. Everything looks so good.

Yeah it does. We will be right back.

Alex and Madison left to go and get food and then came back to the table, both sitting down across from Max as he had already gone through half of his plate already.

Well I guess you were not kidding. You were hungry.

I told you I was. I did not eat this morning. I woke up late. That is why you beat me to work this morning. And thank you for the coffee. So did you find out anything new this morning?

Yes I did, smiled Alex. I love looking on Social media to find out what people are like. Most of the people that we are looking for have a social media account. And they have many pictures usually on their page so I can find out what they do and who they hang out with.

Well that is good. I can always count on you Alex, replied Max.

I am glad that you can. I do the best that I can and with the experience that I have I love what I do. I love being able to get the ones that did it behind bars and keep them there.

So what are you doing this weekend? Asked Madison.

I am just going to relax and clean. I have things to move around and now that it is starting to get cooler I have to switch my clothes around from summer to winter.

I still have to do that too, said Madison. I really do not have as many clothes as I used to before. I got rid of a lot of things when I moved. I just did not want to take it all with me so most of it I donated.

I have to get rid of clothes that I no longer wear, said Alex.

I really need to do that, Max said. Well I think I know what I am doing this weekend now too. It really needs to be done.

So Madison, how do you like it here so far. Isn't this a great find? Alex was happy to come here instead of going to an actual restaurant because they have so much more to offer here. Even though it costs more, the food is great and well it is after all, All you can Eat.

I really like it here. Thank you for inviting me to come. Now I know where we can come again and I will pay. I really do like hanging out with you two especially during lunch time.

Well we really like having you come out with us.

You're both entertaining, Madison said.

Yes we are. We try, said Max.

Well it is easy for Max.

How is it easy for me? asked Max. He was about done with his plate and was ready to go back for Round Two.

Because you have that sense of humor that you're so good at, said Alex.

True I do. Ok I will be back. I think that they are going to have to roll me out of here if I keep eating or they are going to throw me out for eating all of the food. It is so good here.

I am glad that you like it here. Just leave us some food for when we go back up.

Well I might, it just depends. Max left and went up to get more food.

Ok so now that he is gone, it seems to me that you like him, said Madison.

Huh, What gave you that idea?

Just because you spend time together and you get along so well and I see how you look at him. I mean who wouldn't, he is gorgeous. Madison knew as she could tell by the way that they acted towards each other.

We have known each other for quite some time And yes I do like him. He is just so easy going and fun to be with.

That is good. I see that in him. You definitely need someone like him.

Yes I do. My last boyfriend was not good to me at all. I found out that he was cheating on me when I was at work. He was supposed to be at work and I found out that he was off meeting some other woman.

When someone has to do that to someone else then they will do it again and then will do it to someone else.

Hey what are you gabbers talking about? asked Max.

Oh previous boyfriends and why they stay being ex's.

I see. Well you better get up there and get more food before I eat it all.

Are you going back again? Asked Alex.

Soon yes because I still have not had everything yet. This is only an appetizer.

What are you a bottomless pit? Alex laughed.

Yes I am. Replied Max. But there are only a few more things that I want if I have room.

Oh well we are going to go up again at least once more plus grab a desert. They looked good when I was up there looking around. Alex got up and went to check out the food line again.

So what did she do to tell you all of her secrets? asked Max.

About what? No secrets here. Just was talking mostly about her ex boyfriend. He was not very good to her.

No he was not. She was with him when she first started to work with me. And believe it or not he is not with the other girl either. He moved on to the next one. Since then she had not been willing to date. She has been busy with her work. It keeps her mind off of other things and being lonely. I keep her busy. She had asked me to go camping with her and that was a lot of fun. I never really had the time to do it before but she always makes the time to do things and now I understand why she does it. It is very relaxing.

I have never been camping before either. Nothing I have really gotten to do growing up.

Well I cant believe all of the food today. So much stuff that I want to take a little bit of but this is all that I can handle. Alex then sat down and started eating.

Oh you got carrot cake too? Said Max.

Yes it just looked good to me today.

Well I better get back up there. I saw some Chicken before that I wanted to get that looked really good and I did not have enough room on my plate. Why don't they just give us platters instead? Asked Madison.

I really have no idea. I think that they would have to go up in price then for the bigger plates replied Max.

You know I asked that when I go to my family's house for Thanksgiving but no one ever gives me a platter.

I guess Platters are not a thing, said Max.

No, I guess not, Alex replied.

Madison came back with another plate of food and a Cherry Pie.

Oh that pie looks good to Alex. One day I might just come here just for dessert, said Max.

That is not lunch or dinner, said Madison. You can not just eat that.

Why not?asked Alex. Anyways I would still have to eat something besides the dessert because why spend that much money on just desserts?

After lunch they all returned back to the office.

Well we really have to go over the suspects list and figure out what the motives are for Dawn and Sally? I think we already know why Dawn was killed but why Sally?

Could it be because Sally may have seen Dawn's Killer?

Could be, replied Max. I actually think that is the reason why because she knew too much and may have threatened to turn them in.

Ok so we have CJ who would want his wife dead to get the kids, only he is in jail right now as a suspect. CJ's brother Tom is a suspect that we have to get to his house to check his computer. Most everyone has one. Then maybe we can also find out if there is anything written about Sally on it in an email.

Max's phone rang, it was the jail. Oh it must be Samual calling me. Hopefully he found out something.

How did you manage to keep him in jail for now? Asked Alex.

I had talked to Clay. He did a favor for me. Max then answered his phone and went into the back room.

Alex put together the other suspect on the board to see just where they fit in. Then she checked more on social media to see what she could find on their personal profiles. CJ had several and Tom and Tomas only had a few. So following CJ there was so much information on his page. Alex could not figure out why he was posting all of his business on social media. Maybe to make it like he was tough or something.

Max came back to the office. We have very little to go on with CJ. He had bragged about having Dawn killed only to get the children. But as far as Sally it must be the other two because she knew what was going on and she had identified them both as going up to visit her while she was in the hospital. I also think that we need to get search warrants so that is what I am going to go and do now.

Max and Alex left to go and get the search warrants. CJ would be ok since he is in jail right now but the police would have to let them in the house. He would have to call the Sargent to meet them there at the house.

Ok well I have the list of addresses that we need. So we just have to go and get four search warrents. We should be able to go in and take all of the computers and bring them back here to go through. I think that Bill knows how to get into them. He had said that he knew how to get into them before. We need to call him later to let him know that we need him to go through them tomorrow morning.

Yes but first let's just get the computers first.

Max and Alex went to the court house and got what they needed and then left to go to CJ's house. Alex had called for a police officer to go and make sure that they were able to get into the house. CJ is first on the list.

So everyone will be able to come and get their equipment once we are done with it.

Yes, replied Max. We can start going through them first thing in the morning.

We should lock them up in the safe for the night. Call Bill and let him come out and check the devices tomorrow if he could. So that way we can get them checked out.

Sure I can do that now.

Back at the office Max and Alex put the computers in the safe. They did not have time to go through them now.

Well I have written up the reports, saved it in the file on the computer and have a draft ready to send to the judge. Now I am going to leave if that is ok and I will see you tomorrow.. Oh wait, tomorrow is Saturday. Do you need me to come in then? Asked Madison.

No, you can take tomorrow off. Thanks Madison, Max said.

Ok thanks. See you on Monday.

I had forgotten that it was Friday. Well I will still come in tomorrow, replied Max and look at the computers in the morning and then I will take the rest of the weekend off. I just want to check on the computers and see what I find out. So we'll go ahead and leave and go home. I will see you on Monday.

Sure I will see you then. If you need me, call me. I can come in tomorrow if you need me.

Ok but I think I got it. If not, it can wait till Monday. But have a great weekend. Go and relax.

I will. Thanks and I am sure I will talk to you before then. Be careful going home.

Oh I will, said Max. He liked it when she worried about him. But sometimes she worries too much.

Alex went home and put away the groceries that she picked up. She did not need many since she was home for the weekend. She knew that she would be busy and trying to relax before Monday. She decided to eat the salad that she picked up for her dinner tonight. She sat down on the couch and turned on the TV. She found a movie to watch and then remembered she forgot to grab a glass of wine. Getting up she went out to the kitchen and poured her a red wine and then went back in to sit down and enjoy the movie. She texted Max Good night and then fell asleep before the movie ended.

CHAPTER SIX

Alex got up from the couch and realized she did not fall asleep in her bed. She was still on the couch and it was morning. She got up and made a pot of coffee and then got started on the laundry and cleaning the kitchen. Then taking out her summer clothes she decided to go ahead and switch them over and put the summer clothes to the back part of the closet and pulled the winter clothes forward. This helped her to switch out her clothes so that she was set for the winter months. She knew that Snow would be hitting soon enough and she was not thrilled to be driving around in it. Although Virgina really does not get that much snow so she was happy about that part. Nothing like what those who live in the north. She has visited there before and in the winter time and she was so happy that she did not live there.

Alex's phone rang, it was her mom. Oh Hello Mom. How are you?

I am great. Your father went out to play golf with some friends so I am sitting at home enjoying the cooler weather.

Well that is good, replied Alex. I just changed out my summer clothes for my winter ones. Thankfully I do not have a whole lot to change out since it is only me.

That is great to hear, Alex. Oh I want to talk to you about Christmas? We were invited to go out to Arizona this year. Would you mind if we planned on something another time.

Yeah that would be ok. Who are you going to see in Arizona?

Some people that we met on the cruise. They have a big house and asked us to come out and visit. We have a lot in common.

Ok well just be careful when you go out there. These days it is not always safe.

Well they are coming here next summer so we will see how it goes. They do not have any kids or any family there so they invited us to come out. It is warm there at Christmas time.

It is warm in Florida too. It does not get that cold there like it does here.

Yes, well it is always nice to visit other states. Now that we are retired and we can travel it is perfect for us. Besides, we are going there to see the Nutcracker while we are there.

Yeah but mom you can see the Nutcracker anywhere.

I know that dear but we want to go to Arizona to see it there. We are also going to tour some shopping malls while we are there. We always spend Christmas at home. It is just nice to get away for once. I might still decorate here but not as much since we are not going to be home. But anytime you want to come down let me know so I can have your gifts ready. Because I am hoping to be able to do ours early.

Ok well that will be fine. I will let you know when we get the time to go. Only because we have been busy with the new case and we never know what our schedules are going to be like. We even got a call to help with a case and it was in another state but we are busy with this one and we are not able to leave.

Well maybe we will have to do a visit after.

I am hoping that we will not have a case then or even after this one but other areas have been calling us to come out as well to work on cases there because they have a few that they are having trouble with. We may be able to send Bill out instead if we are not able to go. He has a few years on him.

Ok well hopefully I will see you before Christmas. Maybe Max will come with me. Since he lives alone and does not have much family here either.

That would be great. Yes, bring him along. I have the room here for him too.

I will. I don't know when he will go home to South Korea to visit family. I hope he will get to take a few weeks and go to see them because it has been awhile since he has been back there. I have watched some videos of South Korea and it really is a beautiful place. The food there looks really nice and I want to try the food there.

Yes, that would be awesome too. It is always nice to try different foods.

Yeah it is. But then it is hard to find food that is close to being what it is supposed to be. The authentic food. People who actually know how to cook it the way that it should be.

Well anyways I have to go as I have more work to get done so I can relax tomorrow. This week has been a tough one. We have several suspects and we have a lot to go through to find out who the murderer is.

Well I wish you luck in finding out who did it. Please keep me updated.

I will Mom, replied Alex.

Alex had gone and started dinner for herself. She was thinking about asking Max to come over tomorrow for dinner. That would be a great time to have him over because she already knew that he would not want to cook for himself. Then she could send him home with some leftovers.

After she was done with her dinner she put everything away and called Max to invite him over for dinner tomorrow.

Max's phone rang, he saw that it was Alex. He was not surprised that she would call. She usually always called at least once a day if they were not working. She had to check up on him to see how he was doing. Hello. How are you Alex?

I am doing well today. I had a great day. I made a stir fry tonight for dinner.

Oh that sounds good. I should pick up a bag of it to make up when I get home sometime. I do love to make those and have not had them in awhile.

I love them too. I have got this one on sale so I picked up a couple. What did you have for dinner tonight?

I had a sandwich. I was not very hungry tonight. So what are you doing for tomorrow? asked Max.

I am making a Beef casserole. I add vegetables and Noodles in it.

Oh I would like that. I am not picky at all when it comes to food. Replied Max.

So how was your day? What did you do today? Asked Alex.

Not much. I did some cleaning around here and I also went and picked up some stuff that I needed to have to get things done before the week. And I will see you tomorrow. At what time though? Asked Max.

Come on over in the afternoon. I don't care what time. You're always welcome over here. Front door will be open so you can come in when you get here.

Ok will do. I will bring over some wine. Said Max.

Oh good because I am on my last bottle. Bring whatever you want. Said Alex.

I will. I will bring over a bottle that I like. See you tomorrow and have a great night. Get some rest. Said Max.

I will. See you tomorrow. I also have a pie for dessert tomorrow, replied Alex.

Oh wow, there goes my girlish figure then. I will be gaining weight there. Well I will have to work out more this coming week, said Max. He giggled.

Your girlish figure. Is that even a thing for men? Alex asked.

I guess not. But I don't eat much sweets. So anyways I will see you tomorrow.

Alex put the phone on the charger and cleaned up the kitchen and then went into her bedroom, got ready for bed and watched some TV before going to sleep.

CHAPTER SEVEN

Alex got up and made a pot of coffee. She made herself some breakfast and then went in and watched the news. Another burglary in another county to a bank this time. They got away with thousands of dollars. Most of it that was taken was all big bills. The bank owner was upset but insured. She then changed the TV over to a movie and sat and watched that for a while. Finishing her coffee she decided to go ahead and start on the wine, found some cheese and grabbed up the crackers and started to eat them when the door opened up and in walked Max. Alex then realized that she had yet to get dressed and was still in her night clothes. She grabbed up the blanket that was on the couch and wrapped it around her and she excused herself and ran into her bedroom and got dressed. She could not believe that it was already in the afternoon and Max had shown up when she did not expect it.

Alex came back out of the bedroom and saw Max smiling at her. I am sorry I was not ready. I did not expect you to come here so early.

I am sorry. You told me to come over in the afternoon so I did. I thought maybe we could watch a movie before dinner.

Yeah that would be great, said Alex. Pick out whatever you want to watch. There is some cheese and crackers on the coffee table if you want some help yourself. What I was doing was watching a movie before you got here.

It's ok. You looked fine. In my time I had seen women with less clothes than that. That was the hookers that worked the streets. Some were beaten and left for dead.

That is horrible. Where did the girls usually come from? Asked Alex.

Most of them ran away. Some of them came from foster homes, the foster parents had given them to the bad men who then trained them to work the streets. Those foster parents were found and arrested.

I can definitely say I had a perfect upbringing then from what these girls had come from. I am so sorry for them.

Anyways I think I found a good movie, it's a western so come on and sit next to me and watch the movie.

Ok I will get you a glass of wine.

Thanks, replied Max. Let the one I brought get cold for dinner. So what kind of pie did you get?

Apple pie and I got vanilla ice cream.

Oh you sure know a way to a man's heart.

Yes I do, smiled Alex.

I tell you Alex, I am glad that I had met you when you walked into my office that day about the job. It was the best thing that I have done. Not only are you a great worker but you're also a great friend. And I appreciate all you do for me. You and I own the office together because I definitely have found a gem in the pile of nuggets.

Wow, said Alex blushing. Well I learned a lot from you Max. Without you I would not be where I am today.

So let's watch the movie. It has already started.

Ok sure, Alex sat down on the other end of the couch.

After the movie Max found another movie to watch.

Ok well I better start dinner. I just have to put everything together and bake it for a half an hour. I made it before and it was really good. I like to experiment on different foods. Add other things that I like in the casserole and it makes it even better.

Whatever you want to add, go ahead. You already know that I like everything. There really is nothing that I won't eat.

Well that is good. I love everything too. I was never a picky eater when I was growing up. My mom loved to cook for me.

Let's put on some music and go outside to sit while dinner is cooking.

Sure that will be good. We can get some fresh air. Would you like me to start a fire out there?

Yeah I would. I love to sit by the fire. It would be perfect for tonight. The table is out near there and we can sit and watch the fire while we eat.

I really want to have a yard. A place that is quiet. I love it out here. To be able to be in with nature. You're very lucky to have this place.

I know. It really is great out here. No one bothers me here. It is the perfect spot because there are so many wildlife in the area. I love it when the deer comes out in the yard to eat. One mother deer had twins out here the other day.

I have been looking on the internet for homes in the area but none of them have a nice yard with them. I like to have room and I do not want neighbors to be close to me.

Right because then you don't have privacy. There is a lot here and you can't see my house that well from the road. That is another reason why I like it here. No one knows my business.

Well that is true and a good reason to live out where no one knows where you're at or what you're doing. I had actually found one house that I might check out that has land. It used to be a farm. The buildings are still there but they are not being used. I might buy it and then rent out the land. And it is in my price range. I found it this morning actually. I was not going to bother looking at it but the more I think about it, it's a great deal.

That really sounds like a great house. You should go and look at it. Call the realtor tomorrow. You have to go and look at it now before it's gone.

I will. I will put in a request today on my phone for a chance to look at it. Here check it out. It is two stories and has four bedrooms in it. Max hands Alex his phone to look at the pictures.

Well the house really has a nice layout and one bedroom is downstairs. Two big barns and a milk barn. Wow you can even rent out the land for milking if it is someone that is close by.

I will see. I like the land and the privacy of not having any neighbors and I would rather share with cows. I can deal with animals better than people. But that is only if I like the person that is going to put his cows over there. They usually keep them on their own property.

Well either way good luck with it. Can I come and look at it too? I love old homes.

Sure why not. Max put in a request to look at the property tomorrow afternoon. Now I hope that they call to confirm the appointment.

I think Dinner might be ready. I will be right back. I have to check on it. Alex got up and went in to check on the casserole. It smelled good and it has to be close to being ready. Alex opened the oven door and peeked inside. The smell was so good and it did look done. She took it out and checked it on the inside. Yes it was done. Now let it cool down a little before we are able to eat it. Alex went out to the deck to sit with Max for a bit.

Is it done yet? Asked Max.

Yes it is, replied Alex. I just have to let it cool down so we can eat it.

That is why I love your cooking. You're amazing at what you do.

Thank you Max. That means a lot to me.

You're welcome and I don't know why you're surprised because everything you do you put effort into it. You're not one of those girls that just do what needs to be done. You go beyond that. You include me into things that you do. No one else does that for me. I have friends but they are too busy doing what they want to do.

You're my best friend Max. I have to include you and besides you're so much fun to be around. I love being with you. You are great to work with and I have learned so much from you in the past years that we have worked together. I am happy that I found someone that I can feel like I can be myself. It's all business when we are together and if I had been working for someone else they may not have taken the time to work with me like you do.

Thank you Alex. I know that the job is not easy to get to know and that is why I took the time to make sure that you were trained right. You have come a long way from the start and you're a fast learner.Your always going to be my partner as long as you work for me. Because you came on after I opened the department.

Well, let's eat. Dinner should be cooled down enough now. Alex got up and went inside, got two plates and dished up the food onto the plates for each of them.Alex handed Max his plate and they both walked out to the Picnic table to eat.

Wow, another great meal. Thank you Alex. You never disappoint. Thank you again for inviting me over.

You're welcome but you really do not need an invitation. You're welcome here anytime. You know I have the upstairs that I do not even use as I have my bedroom down here. If you want you can move in here. There are a few rooms upstairs that you can use. We can split expenses.

Let me think about that. Can I go up and look?

Sure you can. Go on up and check it out and there is a bathroom up there too. I just decided to take the bedroom down here. The basement is fully furnished too and I use that to make things at.

Max went inside and looked around upstairs. He liked it and the layout was great. He could use one as a bedroom and the other as a den for himself. But first to look at the farm to see just what it has to offer. This would be a great offer as well.

Ok well hopefully we can see what happens tomorrow. I have ice cream for dessert if you would like some.

Sure you know I never pass up ice cream.

Ok well I will take your plate and bring out some ice cream. Did you want more of the casserole?

I will take some more but not too much because I want to eat some pie and ice cream.

I will come in and get the plate so you do not have to bring it back out to me.

No relax I got this.

Ok. Max was not used to being waited on. He was enjoying this.

Alex came out with his plate and then went back in to get some ice cream and then brought them out to the table.

Wow you're too good to me Alex.

Well I wouldn't say that. I just like the company. I like being alone but then I like having someone here too so it would be nice to have someone to come home too.

A roommate would be good. My apartment I pay too much for and have to deal with all that I do there. It is basically the people around that play their music too loud and I just want to rest and relax.

Yes I can relate to that. I once lived in an apartment. All hours of the day and night I kept hearing loud noises. Come to find out one of the neighbors was selling drugs and got busted. That is when I had enough and decided to move in here. My parents wanted to move anyway. So I have the house now. It is the best thing that I have done for myself.

Yes well you have that at least is your own home. So that is always good. Everything is so expensive even if you're married and both working it is hard. How are we able to do this on our own?

It is not easy, replied Alex. At least I do not have a house payment unless I am buying it from my parents which I might do since they are in Florida. I really do not see them moving back here. They are in warmer climates. Mom does not like the cold and Dad just got tired of shoveling snow.

Yes, well at the apartment I do not have to do that. Just a little bit by the door. But they take care of the parking lot.

I pay someone to plow my driveway each winter. I do not have a snowblower. It is just easier to have someone else do it.

That is true, replied Max. With your driveway that is a lot to plow.

Yes it is. So what do you want to do now? Do you want another drink?

Sure I can do one more before going home.

Ok. I will be right back. Alex took Max's wine glass and went back into the house to get more then went back out to the deck with Max.

Well this was a great day today. Perfect weather, perfect company, and great meal, said Max.

Yes it is, thank you for coming out Max. I know you appreciate my cooking. I will send you home some in a bowl.

Ok thanks. I will eat it tomorrow night. This wine is great. What kind is it?

It's Peach on the rocks. That is what it is called because it is also good poured over some ice.

Oh nice. It has a great flavor to it. I was not sure if it was peach or mango.

Well as much as I hate to go I have to get home and relax for tomorrow. Not sure what we have in store for us. Bill has checked in with me about the house, no one has come around at all so that is good. Even though the family had left for a while. I am not sure where they had gone through. Probably to go and see family.

Yeah that would be best and to stay low at their place where they can feel safe.

Ok well I am going to go for the night. See you tomorrow morning. I will bring the coffee.

Ok thanks Max. See you tomorrow.

Max got up and left to go home.

Alex cleaned up the kitchen and went to bed. It was a long fun day.

CHAPTER EIGHT

Alex made it to the office before anyone else. She checked the answering machine and found out that there was another incident at the hospital. This time a patient died from an unknown cause. They will have to do an investigation as soon as Max comes in. Alex decided to call him so that he could go right away.

Hi Max. Where are you? We have another death at the hospital.

What? Another one. Oh no. How did that happen when there was security there?

I do not know but this was a patient.

Oh. This is not good. Three within two weeks.

I am almost there. I have not got the coffee yet. We can get some on our way back through. I will pick you up in a bit. Is Madison there yet?

She just pulled up.

Ok good. I will be pulling up in a minute. Max then hung up the phone.

Hi Madison. We have another case at the hospital.

Oh no not another one?

Yes I am afraid so. This is getting bad. There was a security guard but I do not know what happened to them if they had gone somewhere else or got distracted or what. But they found another patient gone this morning when they went to do vitals on the patients.

Oh well Ok I will be here so go do what you have to do.

Thanks Madison. Talk to you later.

Max pulled up and Alex got in. When is this going to stop? We know who did not do this now but who has done it this timet. I am wondering if CJ had something to do with this but why three people? What is the connection with this one if anything? Alex was puzzled at who could have done this one and why?

Well I hope that we find out something soon because this is the third death. We just have to find out if it was murder or natural causes.

Hopefully Jane is up in the room already.

I do too.

At the hospital Max and Alex went up to the Fourth floor. There was a section blocked off at the room and the other patient had been moved to another room.

Oh good you're here replied Jane. I will have the autopsy sometime this afternoon and will get you the results after. It looks like it is the same case as what happened to Dawn.

What is the patient's name? Asked Max.

Tina Forbes. She is a single mother with one child. She had just been moved up here yesterday.

So we have another single mother dead, replied Alex. Those poor children that have to grow up without a mother. Alex then found a piece of paper on the floor, she picked it up and saw Tina's name on the paper. This paper has her name on it.

I will take it and see if I can get some prints off of it, Said Max.

Is Dawn's husband still in Jail? Asked Jane.

Yes he is. He won't be getting out anytime soon. This must be another hit. Why else would we be standing here with a piece of paper with her name on it. She was a target. Where was the Security guard?

He stepped out to take a break. It has been really quiet up here so the nurses felt like it was ok that he left for a bit. Whoever did this must have come up when he left. There are a lot of hiding spaces for someone to hide in. That is the only problem with this hospital. No matter how secure we try to be, something still happens.

Well they need to do something because this is the third one. I am sure that there will be lawsuits.

There already is one. The nurse that worked here. Her family is suing the hospital. So the hospital is in trouble but they have lawyers for this. Because of the malpractice lawsuits that they get too so they have back up. This is something that was not really preventable at the time.

So what do you think has happened here? Asked Max.

Well that is what I have to find out through the autopsy.

Ok so we will go for now and you can give me a call back later on when you have the information.

I will do that Max, hopefully I will have this done by this afternoon if not it will be done by the morning. It just depends on what I find out from the lab.

Well I will talk to you later.

Ok. replied Jane. Have a great day.

Max and Alex went back to the department. Well now we have to get what information we have into the computer. Can you look up to see if Tina Forbes is on social media Alex. I need to find out if she has something in common with the other two victims.

Sure I am already looking it up online. She has a facebook and I am checking to see who she has as friends. I will see what else she has as social media online.

Ok well let me know what you find out. I forgot to grab coffee. I will run out and grab some coffee. I will try the coffee shop down the street.

Sounds good. Alex went back to looking up information about Tina.

At lunchtime Max and Alex decided to go out to get something to eat. Where do you want to go? asked Max.

We can go to the diner again. I like it there.

Sure we can go there. I like their food there too.

Ok I want to call the realtor first before we go.

They still have not called you back?

No not yet, said Max. But hopefully I can get in today.

Well you can go on lunch to Madison, said Alex.

Sure. I brought my lunch today so I will go back and heat it up. Enjoy your lunch, replied Madison.

We will try. This other death is hitting hard now because we do not know who is doing it.

Ok we can go now and then after that we can go see the house. Madison, we will be back later this afternoon. We may have a call from Jane about the autopsy if she gets it early enough.

Ok I will be here.

Max and Alex got into the car and drove to the Diner.

It was a little busy so they were able to get seated right away. The rush must not have gotten there yet.

Well what do you want to eat? asked Max.

Everything. Are you buying today?

Well if you're eating everything then you're on your own.

Ok well I will just order something that will fill me up then, Alex said with a grin.

Good because I don't want to have to roll you out of here, said Max.

Oh you won't. I will behave. But I'm so hungry.

The waitress came over and took their drink order. They were not ready to order food yet because everything that Alex looked at looked good to her and she had a hard time deciding what to get.

Max decided on the special, it was the soup and sandwich deal. Now that looks good.

Oh yes it does but there are a few other things that I have my eye on too and I just can't decide. Oh this is not good. Well I think I am going to have to go with the stuffed shells with meatballs. It comes with four shells.

Ok well that does sound good too but I am set with what I am going to order. I don't want to be too full to go and look at the house.

The waitress came back with their drinks. Are you ready to order yet?

Yes we are, replied Alex. I Want the stuffed shells with meatballs.

Soup or salad to go with that?

Salad with blue cheese dressing.

And you sir?

I want the special, replied Max.

Ok coming up.

So what are you going to do if you do not like the farm?

Well I will keep looking around. There has to be something out there that I like.

Alex was hoping that he would take her offer if he did not. But all in due time. He may change his mind.

Yeah so hopefully the house will be a great move.

I hope so too, replied Alex. She was hoping that he would pick her place. She loved having him there.

Their food came out and the waitress asked if they needed anything else and then left.

Well this is good. Alex was happy with what she had gotten for lunch. And Max's looked good too.

Wow I really like the Ham and Cheese with the Tomato soup. I love this combo. And yours really looks good. Well maybe I will get that next time.

After lunch Alex and Max drove over to where the house is. Alex was in awe at the beautiful house but her heart sank when she knew that Max would take the house.

Wow this is better than what was in the pictures. And so big. Look at the barns. Are you sure you want to stay doing detective work and not go into farming?

I am sure. I love my job. But I might get some animals to raise. Will probably be most likely beef cows if I decide to get a few. Doing farming is hard and I am not able to do that and do what I do as well.

Ok so let's go inside. The realtor is here.

Just as they were getting out of the car the realtor came out and introduced himself. Hi I am Ryan Marks.

Hello, how are you?

I am doing well, Thanks. Let me show you around the house and then we will go outside to look at the other buildings.

Sure ok. Thanks for seeing us today.

Is this your wife, asked Ryan.

Oh no this is my partner Alex. She works with me.

Oh ok. I was not sure.

They all walked into the front door which led into the living room.

Wow this is nice.

Yes, the owner had the whole place remodeled. So the price is firm.

Ok well I will have to see what I can do then about a loan if I decide to take the place. I like what I see so far.

Over here is the kitchen. It has an open space leading to the dining room. It is big enough to hold a larger group if you have a dinner party.

I see that, said Max. He was happy with what he had seen so far. What do you think Alex?

It looks really nice. But you're the one buying it.

I know but I like your opinion.

The crown molding is what caught my eye when I saw the house the first time. Everything is in such great detail. I love the house myself but this is more for someone who is going to use the farm as a farm. The milking parlor is state of the art. Ryan smiled and walked out to the living room.

Why are they selling?

The husband passed away last year. Wife had to sell off all of the livestock and she went into a retirement home.

Oh that is too bad. It really is beautiful here though. So because of the farm still being a working farm I think I am going to have to think about it.

Well there are some farmers that do rent property for their livestock to be at. They have help come in and milk for them.

That is ok. I had thought about that too but I am not sure if I am comfortable having other people that I do not know on my land. Farmers come in and work the land and leave. But this will make it so that there is someone here all the time. I just am not sure. I will let you know.

Ok well thank you for your time to come out and look at the property. If you change your mind give me a call. Here is my card.

Max took the card, Thank you for the card. I will definitely think about it and if I want to give it a second look I will give you a call.

Yes and the nice thing is that the milk parlor is on the other driveway. So you do not have to share the same driveway if you decide to take the farm.

It is something that I would have to think about.

Max and Alex left to go back to the department. Madison was there still and had just hung up the phone.

Any messages Madison? Asked Max.

Nothing yet, replied Madison.

Ok well thank you. Jane is supposed to call today or tomorrow with results.

Max walked into his office and sat down, checking his emails.

Alex was looking up information on the last victim. She checked social media. She found out that Tina's Family has money. They own a few car lots and Tina had worked at one of them. Alex got up to let Max know the new information. She had to look to see if there was any kind of connection to the others that were killed or even the ones that she had figured had something to do with it. It could be that someone got back at her. I mean she worked at a car lot.

Well we will have to check into that. Lets see what connections she has with the other suspects. I don't think that she would be connected with the ones that were killed. I mean why would someone kill someone that was associated with the ones murdered?

I really do not know but let me check to see who is on her friends list. Alex went back to her office to pull up any kind of information that linked her to the suspects. She did find one. She was friends with Tomas Jones. Well they all have a connection.

Ok so we will have to go and talk to Tomas Jones again. To see where he was last night. Let's ride on over now. Max looked up the address and then got up and they both left to go to the house.

They pulled up in the driveway, Tomas was out on the porch. Alex and Max got out of the car and went up to the porch. Hello Tomas, said Max.

Hello. How are you?

We are good. Just here to see where you were yesterday.

I was at home. I was here with a friend of mine. He came over and needed help with his car.

So you did not go out at all last night?

No I did not. I had a few beers and I do not drive after drinking.

Well that is smart thinking. What about your friend? Asked Max.

He did not drink. He had to go to work after.

Where does he work? Asked Alex.

I really do not know where he works, why does it matter? You're here asking me questions. What is this about anyways?

Tina Forbes was at the hospital last night and was found dead in her room.

Wow really? So what does that have to do with me?

Well since you knew her I thought you might know, replied Max.

Why do you think I had something to do with it?

Did you? Asked Max.

No. I was here all day. I told you that.

Well so far we really do not have any proof that you did not have anything to do with it, replied Alex.

Look, I do not know what to tell you. I was not the one that killed her. Why would I kill her? I really do not know her. She added me on her social media one day. We hardly talked. She added me because I am friends with her then boyfriend.

Who was her boyfriend?

I do not remember. It was two years ago.

Ok well we will be back.

Why? What are you going to try to get me on for? I told you I was here all night. My neighbors knew that I was home. Why don't you go and ask them.

Sure we can do that. And we will, replied Max.

Alex and Max walked over to the neighbors to talk to them. Then came back over to find Tomas had gone inside. They got into the car and left.

Well the neighbors said that he was home all night so that leaves him out. But if he was outside we could have told him what we had been told.

I really can't blame him for being the way that he was though. He did tell us that he was at home and we did not believe him, said Alex.

Well we have to get him talking and hope that he slips up. That is why we do what we do.

Alex and Max went back to the department and Max went into the office to add to his report. Then gave it to Madison to put into the computer tomorrow. It was late and everyone was ready to go home.

Well I will see you tomorrow Max. Have a great night.

You too, said Max.

CHAPTER NINE

Max was the first one at the department and was in his office when Bill came in to give him the latest.

Well we spotted a car in the driveway at the Watsons. But there was no one in it. We checked the house and it was not bothered with. We even checked the windows and they were all locked.

Thank you Bill. You can go ahead and come back to the office starting tomorrow. The Watsons will be gone for a few more weeks.

Ok I will see you tomorrow then. Do you need me to continue with the case that I was looking into?

No, we have to get this case closed. We have to figure out who is the head person on this.

You think that there are more than one? Asked Bill.

Yes there is CJ who I believe is the head person and we have to find out who is working for him. I believe that his friends have something to do with it. But we have to figure out who?

Ok well I will see you tomorrow.

We need someone else to go around and ask questions and Bill is good at what he does. It's not that we are not good at what we do but we need his help on this one. We have to find out what Jane has found out. Let's go see her.

Madison was sitting at her desk working on the paperwork that Max had given her the night before and was putting the information into the computer.

Hi Madison, we will be back later. We have some places that we have to go. And to check out a few suspects.

Sure that is fine. I will be here.

Did you bring your lunch?

Yes I did, Thanks. I will be here until you get back.

Ok if anyone calls that needs us to call them right back you can call me with that information.

I will Max, replied Madison.

Alex and Max left to go to the hospital. They went to her office, but she was not there. They looked in the morgue. She was there working on another body.

Oh glad you're here. I need to show you something.

She pulled the sheet from Tina's body. Do you see this white stuff dried to Tinas lips?

Yes. What is that?

The lab tested it and it came back as Sarin. Somehow someone made it into the room and she had ingested it by breathing it in. They must have had a mask on and that is why they were not affected by it. I believe that Tina was sleeping when they came into her room because she did not have a chance.

Ok but why was the other patient not harmed?

It turns out that she was up walking around and was not in the room when it happened. She had walked down to the waiting room and sat in there watching TV because she did not want to bother Tina as she was not feeling well that night.

Oh so she was more at risk because she was in the room alone. So anyone could have walked in there.

Exactly. Here is your paperwork for your report.

Thank you. Why would anyone go through the trouble to make sure to use other things like this to kill people and where are they getting these things from.

I really do not know. The only person I can think of is a chemist. They would be more able to get their hands on such items. But if the right people get ahold of the items they are able to make it probably by ordering it online.

So we need to find out who is making it. Before more people are harmed.

Yes. Right now.

Ok well we will get right on it.

Max and Alex stopped off at the diner for lunch. Neither one of them could believe what they had just found out. Who would be so evil to do something like this?

Wow I really do not know where to begin on this, said Max.

Neither do I, replied Alex. I will have to go online to find out what it is and where to get it?

Wow what a mess this has become. I am sure that the hospital will be sued for this as well. They should have shut down the floor all together since this is the third murder. It was not anthrax that killed Tina. It was something more lethal.

Well I am not that hungry but I know I need to eat due to us working on this case for the rest of the day. All of this information has just blown my mind. I really do not know where to start on this.

For one start looking up what it is that was used and find out everything that you can about it. I do not want anyone else getting ahold of this or the information. Because I am sure that if it gets out it just might become an outbreak. We have to get these people locked up.

But we really can't without a real cause.

The waitress came over and gave them both a menu and took their drink orders. They both ordered the specials while she was there and she left to get their drinks.

Max and Alex talked more about the case and then changed the subject to the day. It was nice and sunny out.. The diner was not as busy as it was past the lunch rush.

So when are you planning on your next trip out for the weekend?

I really do not know yet, replied Alex. Maybe in a few weeks.

Oh nice. I found a place to go in a few weeks. Up in the mountains at a cabin. I really liked going with you that one weekend. We had a great time.

Well that does sound nice. I have been to the mountains once. The cabin I had rented had a great view.

What was the place called? Asked Max.

Bear Mountain. And once in a while a bear would actually show up there. They try to keep the bears from wandering over in that area but it does not always work. Once in a while they still get in the area somehow.

Oh that is near where I am going to be camping. I am going up to Spring Mountain. I figured it would be nice to get away so I found this place and it has everything that the other place that we rented.

Oh nice. I have heard of Spring Mountain. It is called that because it has a spring running through it. A very cold spring.

I won't be going into the spring but I will be getting some rest and do not have to think about work for a weekend.

Well, have fun. I will be spending time in a hotel again, relaxing up at one of my favorite spots. It has a few restaurants that I like to go and eat at. I make a point to go there at least once or twice a year. This one bar-b-que place is really out of this world.

That is great. I am going to be so lonely without you. I was planning on asking you to come with me but I guess you already have a place picked out.

The waitress came back with the soup and sandwich specials. Alex looked at Max, Yes , I would love to come and join you. Then we can go and look at the falls up there. They have trails that we can walk along and look at the falls.

What about fishing? Do you like to go fishing?

Sure I like to fish. I have a pole and tackle but have not used it in a few years.

Ok well pack your pole and gear then because we are going fishing.

All right. Sounds like a great time.

After lunch Max and Alex went back to the department. Alex got online to see what she could find out if there were any labs or how to make the mixture that killed Tina. She found one an hour away.

Hey Max. I found a lab. It's called Balsh Laboratories. It is an hour away. Let's go and check it out. They do have what killed Tina. Then I think we need to pay CJ a visit.

I agree, let's go.

Max and Alex got up and went out to the car and went to the Lab to find out just what they made and what it was used for. Because someone is getting a hold of them that should not.

At Balsh Laboratories Max and Alex pulled up out front. They went inside and found the main office. A woman was working the desk. Hi, can I help you?

Sure we need to talk to the owner.

He is out on the floor right now. Is there something that I can help you with?

Ok so I am Detective Lee and this is my partner Detective Tibbles. We are here to talk to the owner.

Sure, let me call him. The secretary calls the owner. Yes, someone is here to see you. Two detectives. Ok I will let them know.

He will be right up, he said.

What is the owner's name?

Ralph Balsh. Why don't you go ahead and take a seat?

Sure, replied Alex.

So this is what a Lab looks like? Not bad. It is kind of like one that I had worked in after I graduated high school. I learned a lot there.

Finally the door opened and a man walked in. Hello my name is Ralph Balsh. Can I help you with something?

Yes, can we go somewhere and talk privately?

Sure, follow me to my office. They all walk into the office and Ralph closes the door. Now what can I do for you?

There was an incident at our local hospital where we had three deaths there within a week.

Oh wow. So what does that have to do with me?

Well what was used on one of the patients were arsenic, the other was Serin. The Arsenic was put in through the picc line and the Sarin was ingested.

We make both here but it is for government use. We do not sell to anyone outside of that and everything is locked up after being stored into a sealed room.

Well somehow some of it had left the building. Who do you have working for you?

I have a list here. I will print it out for you.

Do you check their background when they come in to be hired?

Always. We have to do a background check.

Well somehow we think that they had gotten the stuff from here.

Well you have to prove it then. There is no way you can put that on us without any proof.

We plan on doing that. But we have to find out who is doing it. We have a few suspects and we need to find out where they are getting it from.

I can tell you it is not coming from here. They have to be getting it from somewhere else. All of my people have been here for years.

Well lets just hope that we can rule you out. But do you know of anywhere else that would have the same items that we are looking for?

Well there are several here in the States but you have to find out which ones. I am not sure what the names of the Laboratories are but you will have to do your homework on that.

Ok well we will check to see where we go from here. Here is my card if you have any questions or information.

Ok, Thanks I will be in contact with you if I hear of something. And here is the list that you wanted.

Thank you.

Max and Alex went out and got into the car and made their way back to the department. It was almost four in the afternoon.

Back at the department Madison was still there finishing up some work on the computer.

Hello Max, replied Madison. You had a call from CJ Brown. He said that he is moving to the prison soon.

Why is that? He has not been through the trial yet.

I guess maybe he had admitted to something. Anyways, call the jail back and talk to him. He left a number that he was allowed to be reached at.

Max took the number and went back to the office.

I need to have Bill talk to Samual to see if he knows anything yet. People are talking at the jail according to CJ. He is getting nervous because he is afraid that he will be killed in Jail.

Why? They can easily kill him in prison as well. Said Alex.

I know. But I guess that they are able to get a hold of things easier at the jail then they are in prison. This jail is short staffed because they had to bring in more people to the prisons.

I think that they need to close the jails and just open a certain part of the prison to handle these other people.

Not really replied Max. It is out of their budget. But they may just want to close down some of the jails and combine them together.

So who is on the list of people that work at the Lab.

There are about fifty people there, working just twelve hour shifts. I have looked over the list and none of them come to mind of anyone that has ever been into trouble before. But we will have to run a search on them to see if they have a police record.

I can get on that now as I do not have anything going on.

I will stay and help. Want to order dinner?

Yeah we can do that. Wherever you want to get it from. I will start from the middle and work down. You take twenty five and I will take the other twenty five. But what about the owner?

We need to check him out first. He may be trying to pin it on his workers and not even look at him. And we need to check out his secretary too. Do you want Chinese food? I can order from that place down the road.

Yes, that would be great. Whatever you want to order.

Max ordered the food and then started to look up the information on the owner and the secretary first before working on the other workers.

The door opened and someone said hello.

Max got up and went out to pay for the food. Thank you and keep the change.

Thank you sir. Please order anytime. We love the business.

You're welcome and we will.

Max turned around and went into Alex's office and put her food on her desk with a fork.

Oh thank you. Here is my money for the food.

Thank you Alex but you do not have to pay. Keep it for next time.

Ok well it will be my treat next time.

You can count on it.Max left her with her food and left to go into his office to look up to see just what he could find out about the workers. The owner Max had to check out more information. He knew that he had to do some extra digging on the owner as many different links came up with his name linked to it.

Madison popped her head in and said Goodbye as she was done for the day.

Ok Madison. We will see you tomorrow. That is if we get to go home tonight. I am not sure how long we are going to be here going through all the names.

Well get some rest tonight or tomorrow is going to be a long day for you.

We will, replied Max. See you tomorrow.

Max went back to work on his searches. He would go through the rest of the links that are linked to the owner. There were a few that he was interested in. He would have to see what pictures come up with the links to make sure if it is the same person.

A few hours later Alex came into the office and had found nothing on the people on her list. Max was busy still checking out his list and had circled the names on the paper.

How many do you have on your list? Asked Alex.

I have about five people now. But I think that we need to call it a day and go home. We can finish up tomorrow.

Sure that will be fine. I don't think that we really have much going on tomorrow unless something else happens. Alex was tired and was ready to go home and relax.

We really did a good job today. I think we will find our missing link tomorrow on who is getting the drugs and from where. I am pretty sure that it is coming from the lab. Just by some of the things that I have found and have to check out.

Yes we did. I really feel like we have got quite a bit done on these cases and I know that they are all linked together. But why the nurse though? She must have seen something from the first death.

Do you think that she was blackmailing the person? Threatening that she was going to tell if he did not pay her money?

That really could be it. So instead he snuck in and killed her.

Well I am going home. See you tomorrow.

Alex got home and just decided to go into her room and plopped down on the bed. She was exhausted and she just wanted to go to sleep and forget about the day.

Her phone rang and it was her mom. She sure timed it right then as she knows that it is hard to call her during the weekdays.

Hi Mom, how are you?

I am doing well. How are you?

I am doing ok.

Are you busy at work?

Yes we are. We have a big case. We have to find out who the suspect or suspects are. We think that they are all linked together.

Oh, I know that you are not able to talk about it so I will find out after the case is over.

Thanks Mom. It has been some long days. So far there are three victims. But we think it is the same person. That is all I can tell you.

Oh I think I read about it in the paper. Three women at a hospital?

Yes, that is the one. But we have to find out who it is and just who is the mastermind of what is going on.

So how are things going with you and your boss? Anything interesting? She asked.

Nothing new is going on. And if there is, I just want to keep it casual. Nothing more for a while. I just want to get to know him more, which is what I am doing when we go out and do things together. He is my best friend. We have planned on a trip soon to get away and clear our heads and to have fun. I think that we are close to finding out who did it but we have to be sure. I am hoping that someone actually comes forward.

That would be better than trying to figure out who did it. So where are you planning on going for your trip?

Max has rented a cabin up in the mountains and I am going to go up with him. We need a break. So are you going to go anywhere else this year?

Just to our friends house for Christmas. We may take a trip to Hawaii next year.

Oh that will be fun. I have never been there but have heard that it was very nice. I have had friends that went and they had a lot of fun.

Yes I have too. Well I will let you go and get some rest. Good night.

Good night mom. Love you. I will talk to you later on this weekend.

Sure that will be good. Hopefully you will know more about your case by then. I hope that it does not drag out like some of them do.

I know. But anyways I will talk to you later.

Ok. I love you, my sweet daughter.

Alex hung up the phone and went to bed. Mom always worried about her being on the job. You never know what can happen.

CHAPTER TEN

Max got to work first. He wanted to find out just who from the lab had control of the products that they manufacture for these companies. I am sure that Mr Balsh is the main person that is letting someone have access to them. I believe that he is in on it too. But why? Why would he risk everything and lose his business? I just have a feeling that he is going to say that he did not have anything to do with it. Max would have to figure this out soon.

Alex walked in a half an hour later. She walked into Max's office with coffee in hand. Wow, what time did you get here?

About a half an hour ago. I think I know who is the one that is letting the arsenic out as well as the other product.

Who?

It has to be the owner. But he has to be giving it to someone who killed the three women. There must be a reason why he is in it. But what? Blackmail? Asked Alex.

Could be, replied Max. I am sure that could be the reason. Because he has a record for theft when he was twenty-five. He spent some time in prison. Then he went to school and got a degree in Chemistry.

So why would he risk everything if he gets caught.

Someone has to have something on him. That is the only reason why anyone would do something so stupid like this.

What do we do now?

Well now we have to find out who is black mailing him. It has to be that. Why else would he be involved?

Ok so let's go and pick him up.

Alex and Max left to go and pick up Mr Balsh.

Pulling up in the parking lot of Balsh Laboratories there were many cars there. Max and Alex got out and walked into the front doors. The secretary had just got back to her desk.

Hello, can I help you?

Yes we would like to see Ralph Balsh please.

Weren't you in here before?

Yes we were. Now can we please see Ralph Balsh.

Sure let me get him. She picks up the phone and calls his office. Mr Balsh, someone is here to see you in the front office.

Who is it? Mr Balsh asked.

They came in to see before.

Tell them I am not here.

Well they already know that you're here as they are standing at my desk.

Alex and Max looked at each other. They knew that he was trying to avoid seeing them. Now they knew that they had to bring him in for questioning.

Mr Balsh walked out to the reception area. Well hello. Did not expect you back so soon. What can I do for you now?

We need you to come down to our office.

For what?

We need to ask you some questions. To find out where the drugs came from and who took them.

Well I can tell you I had nothing to do with it. But it must be from one of my workers. I am not able to check everyone when they are leaving. They could have taken some home with them.

Wouldn't you know if something was missing?

Not really. We have items that are damaged so we lose some products that way. They are logged in and disposed of.

But what if they were not properly disposed of?

Well they would have to sign off on them. Everything is written down and turned in to me at the end of the day. So far everything has been accounted for.

Somehow something left here. Let's go.

Let me grab my jacket.

At the office Madison was already there. Max had given her own key in case if they were not there when she arrived or if she had to leave she could and get back in. Right this way said Max.

They went back to the big conference office and sat down there talking to Ralph.

So question. Are you being blackmailed?

Why would you ask that?

Because I don't know anyone else with your background that would just throw away a college degree with a great program to think that they would not get caught.

Why do you think I am being black mailed.

Someone knows something and they want you to get them what they want. So who is it? Is it one of the workers?

No, it's someone outside.

Who? Alex asked.

CJ Brown. We knew each other for years. He threatened to tell my wife about my affair that I had a few years ago. He found out about it and he black mailed me. The nurse that was killed is the one that I had the affair with. I hurt my back and had to have surgery. I was on the rehab floor and she was so nice to me. I had asked her out and we were seeing each other for a year.

So Sally was your ex-girlfriend. How interesting. Alex sighed now because a woman was stuck in the middle of a marriage that was not going to end. Most men or women never leave the other as long as they can play the cat and mouse game without getting caught. Only he did get caught.

So why kill her?

Because she saw the person who killed the first woman. The third one I do not know why she was killed.

It is because Tina knew them as well and they had it out for her so they killed her too. All this is because of you. They killed them with your lethal injections.

Yeah but I did not know that the other two were going to get killed. I only knew about the first one.

Well you're under arrest. Please put your hands behind your back and come with us.

Only now your wife will find out about your past and the affair. So where were you saving yourself at then because you're busted now, said Alex.

I need my lawyer.

You can make the call at the police station.

Max and Alex took Ralph to the police station where he was booked and charged in connection with murder.

Well Alex, now we need to go and talk to CJ. He was the head of all of this and the other two just fell into place. The nurse was just a victim because she knew too much. We have to find out who else is behind this. Why should he be the only one going down for what happened? Someone else killed the other two. And I got a call yesterday, the grandparents are back home with the children. They enjoyed their time away with family. The kids got to know more of their family that they never got to see because of CJ. Bill went by the house and made sure that everything was ok. He called me to let me know that the house had not been messed with while they were away.

Oh that is great. Now the kids can finally go on. But without their Mom. So sad but they have her parents to help them remember her. I am sure that they will not see their father or may not even have anything to do with him if he ever gets out.

Yes they will share her memory with them. No matter what, the kids still need their mother but she is no longer able to be here for them. And if the father is not able to care for them then the next best thing is the grandparents.

So what do you want to do now? Do you want to go and talk to CJ?

Let's go to lunch first and then we can go and see him. It might take awhile to get any other information out of him.

To our favorite diner then?

Sure we can do that, said Max.

They both got into the car and drove to the diner.

We will have to ask for a conference room so we can talk to CJ. Did you talk to Bill about his friend that is there to see if he had got any more information from CJ.

Yes I did and CJ is not talking. He does not want to be a part of it even though he already is. Regardless he will be going to prison, I can tell you that right now. And he is not going to like it when he gets in and finds out that he is behind the three women that were killed. Even though he might not have been behind the other two that were killed, he is the reason why it started there.

That is true it was because of him. And he can still talk to them if they come to visit.And I am sure that he has had visitors.

Yes I am sure too. So what are we going to order?

I am wanting breakfast.

The waitress came over and handed them menus and took their drink order. I am sorry you had to seat yourselves. We are short staffed today.

It's ok. We like to sit here at this table anyways.

I will bring some silverware when I bring out the drinks.

Sure that will be great. Thanks.

Max looked over the menu and decided on an omelet with cheese and ham.

Alex decided to get the same but also added broccoli to it.

Oh that does sound good too. We can do both the same.

The waitress came out with their drinks and silverware with some napkins. Ok so what can I get you?

We will have two omelets with ham, cheese and broccoli, replied Max.

Sure I will put that right in for you.

Ok so now we just have to find out who else is working with CJ. We can offer him less time in prison if he tells us who else helped him.

As long as he is confessing he should make it an easier charge for him even though he did not kill the other two. But he was stalking the parents. We can bring him up on charges for that too.

Yes. We will be.I will be putting that all in the paperwork for the Judge.

Their food came out and they were hungry. They needed to get to the jail right after to get CJ to talk.

How is your food asked Max.

It is so good. I do not even cook this well at home for myself. I like to cook for other people but not so much for myself.

I think you do pretty good. You bring me food at different times. You have never disappointed me.

Well thank you. I know you do not get to have much home cooking so I like to cook for you.

At the jail Max and Alex walked in the front door to the front window.

Can I help you? Asked the girl behind the desk.

Yes we are here to talk to CJ. He is an inmate here.

Yes I know who he is. He likes to talk to all the girls here. But he is not my type. He is rough around the edges if you know what I mean.

He is also bad news.

Yeah I know. He is scheduled to leave in a few days. They had to reschedule him as they had an outbreak there but he is scheduled to go out on Monday.

Well that will be good.

Let me get someone up here for you.

Thank you, Max replied.

Alex was looking at the pictures on the wall of the police officers that were currently working there. She noticed a name on the wall. Wow, I have not seen him in awhile. So this is what he is doing. Good for him.

Yeah but I am sure that he is out on the road checking for criminals.

Maybe. Or maybe he is the one coming up to let us in. Alex smiled at Max.

Is he an old boyfriend?

No. But I did like him when I was in highschool. And from his picture he has not changed much.

The door opened and an officer motioned for them to come back.

So you're here to talk to CJ?

Yes we are. We have to talk to him so we might be together for a while. We are hoping that we can close this case soon.

I will have him brought in and I will stand by the door. He has been giving us problems since he has been here. Starting fights is not approved here. Someone finally got the best of him and beat him up pretty good. He is almost healed up but he still runs that mouth of his..

Ok thank you. We will wait here.

I will wait with you. They have gone back already to get him.

Max and Alex sat down on one side of the table so that CJ could sit on the other side. The cop stood over in the corner by the door.

The door opened and CJ came inside. The other officer waited outside the door in case anything happened.

So if it is not the two detectives. So what are you here for to get more information out of me? Well you're not going to get it.

Well if you do not tell us who helped you, you will never get out and see your kids.

According to her parents they won't get to see me anyways. They have them brainwashed so they don't want to have anything to do with me. I did not kill my wife. I don't know who did it but it was not me.

So you think that we don't know that you were not the only one. Come on CJ you had help. Don't tell me this crap. I don't believe you for a minute. So you're saying that you went out and killed the other two women while you were locked up here?

Maybe I did. I make friends.

You do not have that many friends. And from what I hear you're not a hit with the ladies here either.

What are you talking about? Those girls are not my type. They think that they are better than everyone else. I don't like any of them.

You're right there they are better than you. It's because they are not on the other side of the bars where you are.

Yeah you know nothing. And I still am not going to tell you anything.

Oh, you're going to talk. Because you're not leaving here until you do. We can stay here all day. And you're not getting food or water until you do.

Well I got to go to the bathroom. You can't keep me from that.

Oh yes we can. This is how we are going to make you talk.

Oh come on.

Like I said we have all day. And the officer can go home when he is able to. He does not have to stay here.

CJ just sat there looking down at the table and not saying a thing. Even though he really had to go to the bathroom he knew that he could hold it for a while. He was not going to talk.

So CJ where did you get the Arsenic from?

I don't know where it came from. I bought it from someone. It was a one time thing. I had enough to make sure that she died from it. The rest I have stored away to dispose of it later.

Oh but it already has been disposed of.

Well I did not do it. That is all I am telling you.

Come on CJ. You do not want to do this alone. Why? We already know that you have a partner. They have already been picked up.

You're bluffing.

No, they have already been charged and locked up in Prison. He had already said that he has friends there and they will take care of you when you get there.

Why should I believe you? No one said anything about him being locked up.

That is because your other friends do not know yet. And how they do not know is because they have not been able to talk to him yet. We picked him up yesterday. We also picked up your supplier.

Oh really? And who is that?

Not important right now. But he is facing some real big charges for murder. He may not have administered it into the victims but he is the reason why they are dead. So what did you have on him that he had to give them to you?

He had beat up my sister a few years ago. I threatened to send him to jail if he did not do what I asked him to do.

Why wait until now?

He owed me. I kept him and his company out of the news and social media. I had told him that one day I would need him for something. Now his business is going out.

Yes it has already been shut down. It was yesterday after he was arrested.

So that is who you have locked up. He is not one of my friends.

Oh no we have your friend that helped. And well let's say that they are not happy to be there on such charges.

Officer Johnson looked at CJ. Just tell them who else was working with you and then you can leave. You can't leave until you do.

You can't be serious. You can't leave me here. I will make sure you lose your job.

Oh to see you squirm makes me happy.

Come on CJ, I know you do not want to go down as the only one because we already know that someone else killed the other two. Alex wanted him to talk and now.She has been in these situations before and it lasted for hours. But it looked like CJ really had to go so she knew that it was just a matter of time before he went in his chair. And that will get him beat up even more in jail. He still had the weekend to go before he was moved. And she already knew that his roommate did not like him either.

I will go to the board and give them all your names.

We really do not care, replied Max. Give us the name now. I have the bladder of steel. So I can wait all day.

Alright. I will tell you. But I do not want to be in the same prison as him because he is my friend and he will kill me for ratting him out. It was Jack Naples. He killed the nurse and Tina. The nurse knew as much as he was with me when I injected Dawn with the poison. He was my look out and my right hand man. We work together in everything.

Well until now. Now you can be buddies in Prison. That is if he gets put in the same prison as you. Most prisons are filling up now and getting pretty crowded. You may be in a cell with two other people.

So since I told you what kind of deal do I get?

Well if you had not wasted our time here we could have maybe shaved off a year for you but now that you kept us here you get whatever the judge gives you. May you rot there.

I am sure I will get out of good behavior. They are not going to keep me there for that long. Now Jack, that is a different story.

But does he really need to stay in prison? I mean you were the mastermind of it all. Besides, he might kill you while you're there. Just like you said. So you better keep looking over your shoulder while you're there for all three.

Ok well you can take him back now said Alex. She knew that they had the information that they needed and they had to go and pick up Jack. CJ would have company with him at the prison. She knew that he would be there too until they transferred them to another one by next year. They usually rotate the inmates to different prisons if needed to different types of facilities.

Max and Alex left to go and find Jack. Hopefully he was at home and not at work still. They needed to move fast in case CJ decides to call him and tips him off. They pulled up in the driveway and the car was still there. Just then the door opened and Jack came walking out heading to his car.

Going somewhere, asked Alex?

Yes I left something at work. I want to go back and get it. What can I help you with?

Oh I don't know. I think you need to come with us and answer some questions.

Why? I already told you everything that I know.

Well not everything. Replied Max. Let's go.

Just then Jack takes off running.

Max and Alex run after him. Max sped up behind him and knocked Nick to the ground.

Now like I said, you're coming with us. And now we are going to add another charge on you for running away from us.

No way. I did not do anything. It was all CJ doing this. I had nothing to do with it.

Well that is not what we were told by your friends.

Oh so they told you that I did it instead of saying it was them. They were the one that killed the other women. My only mistake was knowing them.

Well you are CJ's best friends.

You mean we were best friends. We are not anymore.

Good because you're going to be spending more time with him.

What? I did not do anything. I want a lawyer.

Oh you're going to get one, replied Alex.

I told you that I did not do anything.

Well you can tell that to the judge.

They got in the car and drove to the police station to turn Jack over to be arrested.

You're going to hear from my lawyer because I am going to sue you and if anything happens to me you are going to get sued for that too.

I am not worried, said Max.

They arrived at the Police Station and walked Jack inside, turned him over to them and then left. They went back to the office to finish up the paperwork.

Hi Madison, are there any messages?

Nope not today. It's been pretty quiet.

So Alex, what do you say after today we take a long weekend and go relax.

That sounds wonderful. I know that we need this time away to unwind. Hey where is Bill anyways? He hasn't reported today?

He is home sick. He thinks he got some bad food at the restaurant so he has been home sick. He called me last night.

Oh wow. I hope that he gets better. Have you talked to him today?

No, I just have not had time. I have been wanting to get this done. Now let's go and get the paperwork done and we can leave. I have to do up the paperwork for the police department and fax it over to them. Then send the paperwork over to the courthouse for the judge.

Max went into his office and got to work on the report, sent it over to the police station and then put the paperwork away for Madison to put into the computer when they came back to work. He then sent the same file over to the Judge via email. Well I am done for the day. Are you ready to take the rest of the week off?

To have Thursday and Friday off and have fun for the weekend. Sure. We are coming back on Monday right?

Sure we probably need to do that. Especially since we have three people in jail right now.

I know we would like to stay away longer but we really need to wait until we get it done and closed.

Yes I know you're right. I will have Bill start on those cases again next week. I will let Madison know that she can take the rest of the week off as she had already left early for a doctor's appointment.

Well I will see you tomorrow, said Alex. What time do you want to leave?

I will call you in the morning when I am ready to go. I am hoping around ten but I will have to see how it goes.

Well see you tomorrow. We will get supplies when we get up to the mountains. That is where we are going, right?

Yes. I will give them a call to make arrangements as they do not know that I want to go up now.

Sure if there are any changes give me a call.

Will do. So go home and pack. See you tomorrow.

Max went home and called the campground. The cabin was finalized for tomorrow. He could not wait to get out in the mountain air to enjoy the cabin especially with Alex.

Alex went home and got to work on what she would bring to the cabin. Wherever they go it would be fine anyways as long as she was with her handsome

Korean Boss. She had gotten used to doing things with him. If he decided to move in she could do a lot more for him. She could not wait.

CHAPTER ELEVEN

Max called Alex to let her know that he should be there around ten. He was just finishing up his packing.

That's fine Max. Oh question. Do you want to check upstairs again to see if you would like sharing the house here with me?

Max had been thinking about this for some time and since it has been so hard for him to be there with all of the things going on at the apartment he really wanted to find a place where he could have some privacy. Yes I can look at it again when I come over and I will think about it. He already knew how peaceful it was there and he liked being around Alex.

Ok great.I will see you when you get here then. Having a roommate would help with the bills. It's not that she is not able to afford it by herself because she can but that does not leave much left over after paying everything. Besides, she will like the company. It has been awhile since she lived with anyone since her last breakup.

Alex grabbed another cup of coffee and made a bagel to eat. Then she unplugged everything that was not going to be in use. Even though she was going to be gone for a few days and Max's car would be out in the driveway it still would look like someone was home. But if he took the upstairs then she would be able to use that as an excuse to why no one answered the door because he did not hear the doorbell. But then again no one really came around the house anyways because it's hidden from the road.

Max pulled up in the driveway, got out and rang the doorbell.

Alex looked at her watch, he was a little early. She smiled and walked over to the door and opened it. Max had on his jeans and tee shirt. His black hair was slicked back like she liked it., She almost melted but then had to remind herself that she was not to do that… just yet.

Well hello said Max. You sure do look beautiful.

Thank's Max. You sure do have a way with words to make a woman smile.

Always. Now where is that room you wanted to show me.

Come on upstairs and I will show you where your living quarters are at. You will have full use of the upstairs.

They both walked upstairs and Max liked what he had seen. He could use the master bedroom upstairs and the smaller one he figured as his den. That way he could watch TV up there and not disturb Alex. He was in awe with the bathroom. It is bigger than the one at the apartment.

Ok so I will think about it. So far I really like the upstairs.

Great. Now let's get the car packed and let's go. I have almost everything in it except for a few essentials.

You're right on top of everything aren't you?

Always. I love to plan ahead.

That is great. That is what I love about you.

Oh and what else do you love about me?

Your cooking of course. And your beautiful smile.

I think we are going to work out great here.

Yes I agree. I do believe that we will. We work well together so we will see how well we can live together. I am sure we will be fine.

Yes I think so too. Well let's get on the road. I am ready to go.

Ok let's finish loading up and we can head out. Did you put your stuff in the car yet?

I am going to do that now. Get the rest of your stuff done so we can go. Do you need help getting the rest of it together?

No, I have a bag almost done so it will be just a minute.

Ok see you out there.

Alex grabbed the bag and finished putting in her essentials like vitamins and stuff, she then zipped it, she shut the lights off and locked up the house. Max was out finishing putting his stuff into the car. Then tried to shut the trunk and it would not quite close up. Max had to move another bag out and put it into the back seat.

Ok now I am ready. Let's go. Are you hungry?

Not yet. We will see when we get close to the mountains. But we can stop and get drinks and snacks for the drive.

That sounds good.

Alex started the car and headed down the road. The store was just up ahead. One of the perks for living close to a small store is that you do not have far to go.

They stopped at the store and got out. Max had noticed a child sitting in the car with another older child. The father came walking out with icecream and handed one to each child, then pumped gas into the car.

Ok well we are almost to the campground. There is a diner up ahead.Lets get something to eat here. It's nice to know that the diner is close by so we can come down here to eat if we do not feel like cooking.

Yes, that is always nice.

Alex parked in front of the diner and they got out and walked in. There were only a few people there eating. Well this is nice. Not many people here and we probably won't have to wait for food. I am starving right now and it smells so good here.

A waitress came over with menus. Hello my name is Julie and I will be your waitress.

Hello Julie. Can we get two cokes please.

Sure coming right up. The waitress left to get the drinks and came back. So are you ready to order?

Not yet, replied Max. He still was not sure what he wanted and Alex was still looking over the menu as well. Although the spaghetti looked good.

Max looked at the specials and saw that the pork roast with mashed potatoes were on the list. Oh wow this looks interesting. I am going to order this for lunch. Always good to eat before you go shopping for food and buy things that you probably won't eat anyways.

Julie came back to see if they were ready to order?

Yes I am. I want the special. Replied Max.

I would like spaghetti with sausage, said Alex. Can I get cheese with that?

Sure I will bring out some for you. I will put it in the order. Is this your first time here?

Yes. We are staying at the campground up the road.

Oh that is nice. It is a great place. A lot of people go there.

That is great. Max found it online. We like to travel to places we have not been to yet. With our job we have to regenerate. It is great to destress so we just go someplace for a few days.

That is a great idea. I have not thought about that. There are a few campgrounds around here that I could take the kids to. Or to even just go to the beach and stay in a hotel.

We have done that too. It's so much fun. And we shopped while we were there. It's a great place to stay. The hotel is amazing.

That is great. I will have to check it out. I will put in your order.

OK thank you, replied Alex. She was hungry.

So we will stop soon after and get some food. Any ideas on what you want to eat while we are there?

Steak, potato and a salad.

I can do that tomorrow, replied Alex. I hope that they have a grill out there.

If not, we can just cook everything inside, said Max.

Yeah but it's always nice to have the food cooked out on the grill.

Yes it is. Either way you're a great cook.

I learned from my mom.

Julie came out with the food. Here you go. Do you need anything else?

I think that we are good for now, said Max.

Ok sure. I will check back on you in a while.

So this looks so good.

Max took a bite of his dinner, it's good but not like yours.

Oh come on. I am not the greatest cook. I like other people's food better than my own. Something about not having to cook for yourself just tastes better.

I agree. That is why I like other peoples cooking more than mine.

After lunch Alex drove to the campground. They stopped at the store first to pick up the key and to pick up supplies for the cabin. Alex asked the guy at the counter if cabins had grills.

Yes we have grills at the cabins. Just make sure that you clean up before you leave.

We can do that. Thank you.

Max and Alex walked around and got their shopping done and then checked out and got the key to the cabin.

Well this is our second Cabin now that we have rented.

Yes it is. It is so nice to be able to stay out here. We will have to check it out like we did the other one to see just what is out here.

I read that there is a lake, we can go boating or swimming. There is another area that is a fishing spot. But I did not bring a pole. Did you?

No. Not this time. I just want to spend it doing some hiking and swimming in the lake. I wanted to go fishing but I decided against it.

That will be fun.

They both got into the car and drove to their cabin, number thirty-eight. It is quite a ways out here. But we will have more privacy because we are almost at the end of the road.

Yes, that is a great thing to have especially when we really do not know our neighbors.

So let's get the food inside and put away first and then bring everything else inside.

Ok. I will grab two bags and you get the last one. I will come back out for the soda.

Ok great. Alex went in with the one bag and started to put the food away in the refrigerator.

Max went out and brought in a few bags of stuff and the soda. So we can choose which bedroom we want. I will let you pick.

No, you go ahead and pick which one you want. I don't care which one I use. We are only here for a few days anyways. Besides, you picked this place out.

Ok well I will leave you the nicer room. Ladies should always have a nice room

Oh, you're so sweet. But really take the nicer room. I don't mind.

Max knew that he could not argue with Alex. She always wins. So he put his bag in one room and her bag in the other room. He went out to help Alex finish putting away the groceries and also finished cleaning out the car of everything that they brought with them.

Is that everything?

Yes it is, replied Max.

Do you want something to drink?

Sure, I will take some Tea.

Ok coming right up. Then we can check the outside. Alex took out two cups and poured Tea into them and then they went out the back door. Outside was a wooded area all around and they could hear the birds in the trees. Squirrels were running around in the trees. A few chipmunks were running from tree to tree. They sat down at the picnic table which also had a grill close by.

Grill looks like it is in decent shape. You can tell it is well used. Glad you asked so that we could pick up the charcoal at the store.

Yes, nothing like cooking out on the grill. The burgers just taste better on a grill.

Yes they are, replied Max. Your burgers are the best.

Oh you're just saying that Max. Alex grinned. Don't worry I will still make you dinner.

Well that is good otherwise I will have to make dinner and you don't want that.

Why not you are a great cook, replied Alex.

Well sometimes. I do well with certain things. Your hamburgers are great. Where did you learn to cook like that?

My dad did most of the grilling while my mom did most of the cooking on the stove or oven. Both of my parents loved to cook.

That is great. I am glad that you learned how to cook from them.

Yes, me too. What did you learn from your parents?

Well it was not much from cooking but I learned how to take care of myself. You can teach me cooking.

Yes I would be glad to help you with that. And anything else that you need help with.

So let's just relax here and enjoy ourselves. I will help you with the cooking while we are here. I like to learn.

Sounds good Max. Thank you. I will show you basic cooking while we are here. Cooking is basically easy if you read the recipe right. I would start out with basic meals like spaghetti as you can use jars of sauce and some kind of meat. Hamburgers are easy to do, hotdogs are easier because you just cook them in a pan or on a grill. Steak is also another easy meat to cook. There are others that you can put into a crock pot to cook. But that will be later on to teach you that.

Ok well those seem easy enough. I look forward to learning. I do cook hamburgers inside but I never seem to get them seasoned like you do. Hotdogs are easy to do as I just fry them up in a pan and eat chips with them. I have done boxed macaroni and Cheese. Even Spaghetti with just jars of spaghetti sauce but I have not done much with pasta dishes. My mom had always cooked for me. I go over sometimes when she has me over for dinner. I really did not learn how to cook the basic things because she always cooked for me. She always felt that it was the woman's thing to do because she always cooked for everyone.

Well it sounds like you have some cooking skills to cook. I always felt that it does not matter if you're a man or woman, everyone should know how to cook because one day you might be having to do it on your own. I like to cook for others but I feel that they too need to know how to cook on their own.

Well enough on that. I want to enjoy the outdoors. Then we can start up the grill and start cooking those burgers. You know what we did not get though.Is a bottle of wine.

Oh I brought wine. I put it in the refrigerator already.

Awesome, thank you. I like your choices of wine. I usually drink beer but I also like wine.

I do drink beer sometimes. But I like the wines better.

Well that is good. I am not sure what most women like to drink, most that I have been with like to drink beer. A few liked to drink wine but with meals. I had one woman that did not drink at all. I was fine with it but she did not like it because I drank. Her father was a drinker.

Well that had to be hard for her. My Uncle, he drank all the time. He would come home and start drinking. But that was him. I really am not to judge anyone. He was a good uncle but he would sometimes get mean when he drank.

So I have to mention that I am hoping to go to Korea next year. To see family that I have not seen in quite some time. So I need to save for the trip.

How long do you plan on going for?

I am hoping for at least three weeks. Bill can handle it while I am gone. If things work out would you like to go with me?

Yes I would. I love to learn about other cultures. I learned Spanish when I was in school. I want to learn other languages too. When did you learn English?

I learned it over in Korea in school. It is one of the languages that most people learn in elementary school. We have teachers that come over from here in America that go over to Korea to teach children how to speak english.

Wow, that is amazing. I never knew that they did that.

Yes, the teachers come to Korea and they stay at the places provided by the school and they are there for maybe a few years depending on how long their contract is.

Do they stay there for a long time?

Most come back to America. It is a great learning experience for them. But some of them stay as a resident, they have to reapply again for residency to stay in Korea. If they are married it does not guarantee that they are going to stay there just because they are married, they have to recertify for citizenship when their's expire.

Oh wow I did not know that.

I actually miss not living there but I like it here too.

Well that is good. I am glad that you like living here. Besides your parents are here

Yes and I am glad that they are. How are they doing?

Oh they are doing good. They went to Korea to visit family and they are back now. I went to see them the other day.

That is great. Hope that they had a nice time there.

They did. They got to visit with a lot of the family there. They all got together at my Uncles and stayed there for the time that they were there and many of the family members came and visited with them. My Uncle lives outside of the big city there called Seoul but they got to go there to do some shopping at the mall and to walk along the Han River. My parents love it in Seoul. They miss it. They used to live there and they love Han River.

What else is there to do? Since I have gotten to know you I have looked up South Korea and found many things that I would like to go to. One being the big event for cats at the cat fair.

I have not been to that but I have heard about it. They have everything there for cats that are handmade by different people. I would love to go sometime just to check it out. Have you ever thought about getting a cat? Asked Max.

I have but I am just not home enough except for on the weekends.

Well they are quite independent and make great mousers. So leaving them at home for a few days is ok. If you were going to be gone longer maybe see if you can have a friend to come and stay with your kitty. House sit.

Yeah we had a cat when I was growing up. It was heartbreaking when she died. I have had her since she was a kitten. Just hard to lose an animal.

I understand that, replied Max. I lost a dog that I had rescued. He was left behind in a vacant house. He was so skinny when I finally was able to get him out of the house. The landlord came and opened the door for me.

Wow well I am glad that you were able to save him when you did.

Yes, me too. He was a great dog. I named him Lucky because he was very lucky to still be alive.

Well I am going to go ahead and start dinner. First I want to get the grill going so it can get hot enough before I start cooking. I am also going to put some foil down on the grill before putting the meat on. Steak, baked potato and mushrooms?

Yes, that is great. I will start the grill, said Max. He got up and grabbed the charcoal and lighter and started the grill.

Alex went in and grabbed a bottle of wine out of the refrigerator and poured more wine in her glass, then took out the steak and seasoned it, then put two baking potatoes in foil and wrapped them up. She then took the mushrooms and put them on a piece of foil, added some butter, salt and pepper and wrapped it up. Then she put everything on a plate and took it out to the grill.

Oh the steaks look good, replied Max.

Yes, I put some steak seasoning on them. I love this seasoning. Alex placed the steaks that are on the foil onto the grill and then the potatoes and mushrooms on. The steaks started to sizzle and Alex took in the wonderful smells of dinner.

That smells amazing Alex.

I am glad, hopefully it tastes as great as it smells.

I am sure that it will. Max was taking in all the smells of the food cooking. He could not wait to eat.

Ok well it is almost done. The steaks have to cook a little more. I will leave the potatoes on for a bit longer before taking them off. We have sour cream to put on them.

Oh yes I remember that we got it. I had actually forgotten about it. We got a lot of food for the weekend. Snacks. Can't go wrong with snacks.

For sure, and wine, said Alex. She was happy that they both are doing this weekend. Alex always loves getting away and she looks forward to her trips. It's nice to be at home but it is even better to be able to get away for a weekend.

Ok so Dinner is ready. Let's eat. Max could not wait. He was starving, smelling all the food cooking.

Alex grabbed the plate and put the food on the plate and placed it on the table. Alex went in to get everything and brought them out to the table. Max waited until Alex got her food before getting his because it was just a respectful thing to do. He was thankful that they were out at the campground. There were not as many people out and the cabin next to them was not occupied.

Sitting down at the table Alex cut into the steak and tasted it. Oh wow this is good. Perfect grilling.

Yes it is, Max replied. Five star cooking Alex. Thank you.

Your welcome kind sir. I mean I know that I am not the best cook but I like what I make.

Anytime. I never turn down a home cooked meal.

Neither have I. My mom is the best cook. She has learned so much from my grandmother.

After dinner Alex cleaned up the kitchen and washed all the dishes. There were not many since they used the grill. She went back out on the deck and sat down with her wine and handed Max a glass of wine as well.

Thank you for dinner and for coming out here with me. I enjoy our time together. I know we spend time at work a lot but this is different. At work we are a team. Outside of work we are friends. And I am considering the idea of renting out the upstairs. Since there are three bedrooms I want to make one like a multipurpose room. Someplace that I can go to give you your space. You know in case you have friends or family over. I do not want to be in the way.

My house is your house. You do not have to go upstairs to give me privacy.

I am more of a private person when it comes to people outside of work. I would rather just be in my own space.

Well ok then. We can do it that way but I really do not have many friends that come over except for one. And she stays busy with work and her husband. I wonder how their trip went. I will have to call her sometime.

Hey, look over there. Max was pointing to the edge of the woods. There stood a mother deer and a baby. I love it out here already. Anyplace to go to relax with Deer is amazing. I love Nature so much that I really regret moving to the city area but it was the only place I could find at the time.

Well the Mother deer noticed us because we are talking, we have to be quiet or she will go into the woods. Oh too late there she goes with the baby.

Max and Alex sat outside for another hour before going inside and starting a fire. Alex decided to read before bed. Max sat listening to music on his phone. Alex was getting sleepy and got up to go to bed.

Well I am going to bed. I will see you in the morning. Have a great night.

You too. I think I am going to turn in soon too. Just want to listen to some more music before turning in. Max got up and took both wine glasses and walked over to the kitchen sink, washed them and put them into the dish drainer. Put out the fire and then shut off the lights.

CHAPTER TWELVE

Alex woke up the next morning and took a shower. Then she went out into the kitchen and made a pot of coffee. Max was still sleeping. She took out the eggs and bacon and started to make breakfast. She had looked at the weather report on her phone. High in the seventies and sunny. Well that was going to be a great day then. Not too hot. She wanted to go down to the lake and go in for a swim.

Max came out of his room and walked out to the kitchen. Oh, something smells good. Do I smell bacon? And coffee?

Yes. I had thought that the smell would bring you out of your slumber. How did you sleep?

I have no clue. I did not stay awake to find out.

Alex laughed, well I didn't either but I am well rested. The bed was perfect.

Yes it was. I mean my bed was too. That just sounded weird.

Alex would not have minded if Max had slept in her bed with her. But that was her secret. She knew that one day they would be together. She knew that it would take some time.

So I am going to get a shower. What do you want to do today?

Well today would be a perfect day to go down to the lake.

Oh yes, great idea. Don't let me forget to put on sunscreen.

I won't forget. Breakfast is almost done.

Ok I will be quick with my shower.

Take your time. I will keep it warm for you.

Thank you Alex.

Alex grabbed a coffee cup and poured herself some coffee. She got out the coffee creamer and put it in. She did not need sugar because the creamer is already sweet. The eggs and bacon were already done and she kept it in the pan to stay warm. She put some cheese on the eggs and let it melt. She could not wait to eat because it smelled so good. She got a chocolate chip cookie and ate it because she could not wait to eat.

The door opened and Max walked out in shorts and tshirt. He smelled so good. What are you wearing?

Hopefully Clothes. Max laughed. What do you mean what am I wearing? You mean the cologne?

Yes smartie. Alex grinned at Max. He has a great sense of humor.

It's Chanel for men. I like it alot.

It smells really good. Said Alex.

Thank you. Maybe I should wear it to work too, Max smiled at Alex.

Oh but I probably will not get any work done.

So I shouldnt wear it then?

It's up to you, if you want any work from me that is.

Wow, who knew that smelling good would drive you wild.

Well I wouldn't go as far as wild. But I do like the scent.

Good to know Max said. Now about breakfast.

Oh yes, sit down at the table and I will bring the food to the table. She poured a cup of Coffee for Max and brought it over to him. Then she put the eggs and bacon on two plates and brought them over to the table and set one plate in front of Max.

Oh this smells and looks great. Thank you Chef Alex.

You're welcome, you're the best customer that I have.

Max ate without saying another word until he was done. Oh this was the best.

Thank you. Glad you liked it. It's one of my favorites to make.

Well it is also one of my favorites to eat because it is just simple. But I do like Omelets as well with other vegetables and meat tucked away in them.

Yes I love them too. But even more when someone else makes them.

Do you want another cup of coffee? asked Max.

Sure, Thank you.

No thank you for doing this. Usually I don't eat anything unless I eat Cereal.

I like cereal too in the mornings. Usually when I do not feel like making anything, which is most of the time. But then there are those days that I just pick up breakfast.

Yeah, why did we not pick up some cereal for our trip?

Because I like to cook breakfast when we are out in the cabin. I have more time to cook then.

Yes but you do not want to spend the whole weekend cooking. It's always nice to go out to eat too. Or I can cook something. Believe it or not I can cook eggs but I usually do the eggs sunny side up.

Oh yes I like them cooked like that too. Ok enough about food, let's go outside on the deck and drink our coffee and then go to the lake.

Sure. It will be a nice walk down there. We will have to check out later on just what else is around here. I hear kids playing someplace.

Yeah I do too. But only a few.

Down at the lake it was not that busy with kids and adults. I think it is still early yet for others to be coming down.

Yeah maybe. Well I am going to go in for a bit but only going to walk in. I am not going to go swimming. We will find something to do after lunch.

Ok sure. Alex took off her shoes and walked into the water. It was cold and clear. Kids were in the water playing with a beach ball. Others were playing in the sand. The sun was out and shining brightly on her face. She loved it here. It was a great place to be. The whole campground was just amazing with the way it was laid out. There were canoes that people could just go out on. There was a volleyball area and there were some teens playing. At the store it was busy with campers. Children were running around outside chasing each other.

Max got out of the water and went and sat down on a bench to dry his feet. Alex got out and walked over and sat down next to him. Well what do you want to do now?

Let's go to one of the parks and look around. Or go for a drive. We can do our own tour around here.

That sounds great. Then we can stop and get something to eat and figure out what we want to do from there.

I will look on my phone to see what there is to do today. Alex got her phone and checked out the area. She found a place on the other side of the lake that has concerts. Would you like to go check that out? They will be doing one at Two o'clock this afternoon. I think that we can get a snack and go there and sit. Let's grab a blanket from the cabin and then we can stop at the store and get some snacks and drinks.

Back at the cabin Alex went in and got a blanket, she brought an extra one just in case she got cold. She then went to the car and got in and they both went to the store to get what they needed. Then it was off to the concert. By the time that they had arrived it was already filled with concert goers. Children were playing together and there was a hotdog and hamburger stand with drinks.

Oh we could get lunch here. Who knows how long we are going to be here for so we got the chips to go with the food. Let's go.

Why don't you stay here and save our spot. I will get the food. One of each?

Sure but cheese on the burger. Ketchup and pickles.

Ok I will be right back.

Alex spread out the blanket on the lawn and sat down with the bottled water and chips.

Max came back with two hotdogs and two hamburgers with cheese. Here you go my princess. Enjoy.

Princess? Alex smiled.

Yes while we are on our mini vacation you are my Princess.

Ok then you're my Prince.

That sounds fair enough. Let's eat.

So I wonder who is playing today?.

I don't know. Let me check on my phone to see who it is. Alex looked on her phone and the website said TBA which meant to be announced. Well that does not tell us anything.

Well they probably are not able to book too far in advance with these things you know. People might change their minds on if they are able to perform or not.

These are pretty good for concession stand food. It's not how it's made but what it is made from that matters and they really got the good meat. They also had sausage as well but I know that we wanted these so that is what I got. Besides, the Sausage was a few dollars more.

That is ok. I like what we got

They finished their food and Max threw away the garbage and came back to sit down. The band came on stage to perform.

Hello everyone. Thank you for being here. We are The Swinging Crabs. We appreciate all of you for coming out. Please feel free to dance if you want. We are here to make you happy today. They started out playing a song from Alabama Song of the South. Everyone clapped and sang along to the music. Towards the end of their performance they decided to sing Elvis Jailhouse Rock. Everyone was having a great time and wanted more. The band left the stage and the announcer came back on the stage. Thank you everyone and I hope that you had fun. We have another treat for you. The Crunchy Tacos is here to perform music tonight as well. While they get ready to set up please take this time to get something to eat or to use our facilities. Enjoy the night. And please before you leave take your garbage that is located near the food booth.

Do you want anything else? Asked Max.

No, I am fine. I still have my water left.

Ok great. Let me know if you need anything.

I will, Thanks Alex.

Just then The Crunchy Tacos came on stage, set up their equipment. Thank you all for staying here to listen to us sing some oldies. We are going to start with some songs from Pink Floyd and then end it with The Beatles.

Everyone in the crowd clapped as the singers started singing Another brick in the wall which is everyone's favorite. Everyone was up dancing to the music and clapping. Then the band went to play some Beatles, Get Back. Everyone was singing along. Once everything was done everyone got up to leave and there was no garbage left behind. That is a great thing that people do here to keep the park clean.

Well let's go and find something to eat, said Alex.

What about the diner?

I think that I saw a seafood restaurant on our way here.

Oh yes I did see that replied Max. Well let's go then. What about a campfire after?

Yes we have some firewood on the back deck so we can build a fire and sit outside. That sounds nice. A perfect ending to a perfect day.

Max was happy that they had gone to the outside concert and now went out to a nice dinner. Then he could get a glass of wine in him before bed. He was glad that they were getting to know each other more outside of work. Alex was more relaxed outside of work. There was just too much going on at work. He liked the relaxed side of Alex.

At the restaurant Max and Alex walked in and the place was crowded. Looks like everyone else had the same idea. Do you want to go or stay?

Well, let's stay. We are hungry for Seafood.

A lady came over and got their name and told them to take a seat.

Max and Alex went over to the waiting area and sat down. There was a group of people ahead of them.

Are you sure you want to stay?

Sure replied Max. What Alex wants, Alex gets. Hey, you're my best employee. I have to keep you happy. Because if I dont you will go somewhere else.

No I won't. I like where I am at. I love working with you. I have learned so much from you.

Yes you have and you follow the rules as well which is good because my other partner did what he wanted to do. You know when you applied I was skeptical at first as I have never worked with a woman before on cases. But there was something about you that I liked. You are real, you know what you want and you go for it.

That is true. I have always gone by the book in any job that I had. Not everyone does because they like to find the easy way around things.

The hostess came over to let them know that their table was ready. They got up and followed her to a table with a window.

The waitress came over to get their drink order. Hi my name is Ginger, I am so sorry for the wait. Since the concert let out we have been busy. What can I get you to drink?

Two Iced Teas please.

Sure coming right up.

Tea with Seafood. I would have figured beer or wine, replied Max.

Well we are going to have wine when we get back to the cabin so I don't want to drink wine here.

Ok well that is ok. What do you want to eat for dinner? Max looked over the menu getting more hungry looking at all the great options with the list of sides.

I don't know. There is just so much to pick from. What about the seafood sampler? It has Lobster Tail, Crab and Scallops with a baked potato.Alex was very hungry by now.

Yes that does sound good, said Max. I think I am going to pick that too. Baked potato with sour cream.

Oh yes. With extra melted butter.

The waitress came over with their drinks. Are you ready to order? she asked.

Yes we are going to order two Seafood samplers with Baked Potato with sour cream with extra melted butter.

Ok sure, coming right up.

She got the menus and left.

Ok so we eat and go back to the cabin and relax with a glass of wine. What else do we have?

Max, do we really need anything else? We have enough food here and I am not sure if I can finish it all tonight. I might have some for tomorrow.

You're right. I am just used to snacking on stuff before bed. It's because I really do not have anything else to do before bed except watch tv and then I watch the news and then I go to bed.

Do you have a TV in your room? I have one in my room especially since I am not able to go right to sleep.

No, I like the quiet replies Max.

So what do you want to do tomorrow?

Oh I don't know. Maybe stay at the cabin and enjoy the peace out there. It is definitely peaceful there.

Sure we can do that. We are here to rest anyways so that is what we can do. Take a day and just hang out at the cabin. I will grill the sausage tomorrow if you want.

Yeah that is ok. Max looked down at his tea and took a drink. I am so hungry right now.

Same here. Oh I think our food is coming now.

The waitress came over with their food and put it on the table.

Oh this smells and looks so good.

Enjoy. Everyone that comes in here says our food is the best. And I have to say that it is because I eat here all the time. Well, enjoy. Let me know if you need anything. There is cocktail sauce on the table if you need it.

Ok thank you. Alex picked up her fork and picked up a scallop and dipped it into the butter and took a bite. Oh this is amazing.

Yes it is replied Max as he put a fork full of Lobster in his mouth. Oh this lobster is the best. I have never had anything so good. Guess this is why they were busy earlier.

Well there are still people coming in.

Well I am too hungry to talk. I want to learn how to make this.

I always google different recipes to find out how to cook things and usually it always turns out great.

Max was busy eating and really did not want to stop to talk. Food is always a way to a man's stomach and heart.

After dinner Max and Alex headed back to the campground. Well this was a fun day, said Alex.

Yes, replied Max. It's starting to get chilly out so it will be nice to sit by the fire. Maybe make some smores.

Oh yes I have some chocolate that I brought with me in case we wanted to do that again. I thought that we would want to have them out here. I will bring out the stuff if you want to get the fire going please.

I sure can. I am having so much fun out here this weekend. It's great to have someone to do things together as much as we do, we are both compatible together.

Yes we are. You are amazing to hang out with, said Alex. And you're great to work with. That is what makes us a great team.

Once I get more people in we will be much better as we can take on more clients. I have been doing a lot of thinking and I have made up my mind. I am letting you take charge of hiring people to help grow our team. I am making you a partner in the business. We have to hire people. But we are going to have to expand our building so that we can grow.

Are you serious? Do you really want me as a partner? I mean this is your baby.

Well it is both of ours. You work hard just like I do. That is why we do work well together because we are a lot alike.

And I need backup in case you're sick or if I am and need time off. That way our clients are not waiting until we get back, someone else will be able to help them. I want to hire twelve more people so that we can have a good working team. Then later on we can see how many more we can work with. We can handle more cases this way.

Yes I agree. But have me hire people. Are you sure?

Yes I need time to watch over everything else. So I am leaving you in charge of that. Use your intuition for the hires. If you feel that they are a good match and check out their background then hire them.

Wow, thank you. Yes I can do this. We are a team. I appreciate your confidence in me.

You're welcome Alex. You earned it. Now let's make some smores.

Alex went over and gave Max a hug. She was so happy that he trusted her to make her a partner in the business. She loved her job and she was good at it. She was falling for Max even more.

Max had wanted this more than anything. It was then that he had kissed her. He was glad that he had made her partner and he had hoped that he was doing the right thing. He felt that he had done the right thing. He did not want to damage what they had together.

Alex could not believe that he was kissing her and she just melted as she kissed him back. He was the best kisser that she had ever had. She started to feel dizzy and had to sit down.

Are you ok? Asked Max.

I am fine. Just a little dizzy. All this has become too much for me.

I am sorry. Can I get you anything?

No, I will be fine. Let's just get the S'mores done. I just have to process all of this. I am glad that we are on a trip and not at work. So I have a few days to take this all in. And for the kiss it was amazing. I have been wanting this for a very long time. I just did not want to say anything because I was not sure how you would take it and I did not want my heart broken again.

I have been having these feelings for you for awhile.And I am glad that you feel the same way about me.

Max you are the most handsome man I have met and to be honest I have liked you since I first met you. I just did not want to go any further until now. We have been great friends for so long. You are like my Ying to my Yang.

Wow I never thought about it that way. You're right. So next week I will start packing up my apartment and start moving in next week. What do you say?

That would be great. Now let's cook the marshmallows. Alex put a few on a stick and toasted them in the fire.

Max got the graham crackers and chocolate put together for the marshmallow to go on. Alex put a marshmallow on each piece of chocolate then put two more on the stick. How many can you eat?

A few. I am still full from dinner. Thank you.

You're welcome. Alex was glad that he was so easy to please. Max does not ask for much and does not demand much from their job. She was good at her job and she loved it.

So what about tomorrow? I know that we are going to hang around the cabin. What do you want to do?

Alex could think of many things to do. But she did not want to rush into things as much as she wanted to. All of this was what she wanted. And she wanted to enjoy each day with him even more. I think that we can just hang out here tomorrow and see what the day brings. Let's just enjoy the wildlife if we see any.

Ok sounds good, said Max. We can just relax. That is why we are here. To relax and clear our minds.

Yes well we are definitely doing that. This has been a great few days. Spending time with you is always fun. I am glad that we can do this together.

Sure, that is why we work so well together. We get along like Peanut butter and Jelly.

Yes we do. But what kind of Jelly am I?

Um, let's see. Strawberry. I like strawberries.

Yes, I like strawberries. I also like Peaches.

Hmmm. Peach. Nah, I like strawberries better. Max smiled and went to get another glass of wine. He brought out the bottle and poured some more in Alex's glass.

Thank you Max. You're so sweet.

You're welcome. Anytime. Max sat back down in the chair and finished his Smores.

Max and Alex sat out looking at the moon. The fireflies were out lighting up the area. It was so pretty. The night sparkled. They finished their wine and went inside, Alex cleaned up the kitchen and then they both decided to call it a night.

Good night Alex. See you in the morning. We can sleep in with nowhere to go.

Yes we can. Good night.

CHAPTER THIRTEEN

Alex got up and listened. She heard Max out in the kitchen. Well he was the first one up this morning. She went in and got a shower and then went out to greet the morning.

Good morning Max. What do you want for breakfast?

Sit down. I am making breakfast this morning. I had already started the coffee. He got out a coffee cup and poured coffee in it and brought it over to Alex.

Thank you Max. How did you sleep last night?

I slept well. I was so tired from everything that we did yesterday but I had a great time. The concerts were amazing. I am glad that you found that. It was a great day to do it too. Perfect weather.

Yes it was. And the dinner after was great. I really wish we had someplace like that close to home. But we can come here again.

Sure that would be great. Max smiled. Now what would you like for Breakfast?

Whatever you want to make is fine with me. Do you want any help?

No, I got it. It is my turn to cook this time. I can make some scrambled eggs and toast. I will even put cheese on them. Just the way you like them.

Thank you Max. Then I will clean up the kitchen after.

I can do that too, replied Max.Just relax this morning. I got this.

Alex smiled and watched Max as he prepared breakfast for them. I really appreciate this.

No Problem. You don't have to be doing everything. I can help too.

And I appreciate that. But you do not have to do it. I like to do these things.

I know and I just want to help. Why can't you just let me help to do things.

I guess I have been doing it for so long I just got used to it. I just do not know what to do with myself but to do these things.

You will make a fantastic wife then, Max smiled at her.

Well I don't know about that. I am nothing special. I am just like everyone else.

Well yes but you are more mature than most of the women that I know.

Yes I agree on that. Most are still trying to figure out what they want to do and some just do not want to be anything else. Some just do not take the responsibility.

I think a lot of it is that they are still trying to find themselves and what they want to do. Many go to college but more are just trying to find out what they really want to do.

My sister was the same. Then she got married and then went to college online to do business. I went to college after I got out of school for Criminal Justice. The more that I was doing in school my sister decided to go online for her degree. She was married and was starting a family so she wanted to do her schooling online.

Well that is great. What does she do now? Asked Max.

She is an accountant for several businesses near her home. She loves it. She had told me that she wished that she had done it sooner.

Well I am glad that she likes what she does. So is she able to work when she wants?

Most of the time. Her husband has certain days off so he can stay home with the kids while she goes to the other places that she needs to work on.

It was getting close to lunch time and Alex was getting hungry. What would you like for lunch?

I really do not care. I am not hungry yet.

Ok I will just get something to snack on then. Alex got up to go to the kitchen and got some Cheese crackers. I had forgotten about these.

Oh yeah I did too, replied Max.

Alex brought the box over and shared it with Max. Men can eat. She knew that he would want to have some as well. Max never turns down food.

So are you still happy that we are taking the day to relax. Tomorrow morning we can pack up the car and then wander around one last time.

I don't know. It might be nice to go for a walk later. Before dinner that way we will be hungry. Alex really did not want the weekend to end. Spending this time with Max was wonderful and fun. Monday would be back to the office and working the case again. Hopefully the trial will be soon and the case can be closed.

Have you talked to Bill lately?

Yes on Thursday morning. He said that he would be at the office Monday morning and working on a cold case that he wanted to reopen. He has a lead on it.

Oh that is great news. Hopefully we can finally get answers to the family. Ok now let's enjoy the great outdoors.

Oh look Alex, over there by the edge of the woods. Do you see the deer with the babies?

Yes I do. Oh look the babies are eating and the mother is watching us. I don't think that she will let them come out since we are sitting out here.

Probably not. But I am just going to sit here and not get up because it might spook her and the babies. Twins, how cool is that. They both have their spots still.

They both sat there quietly watching the deer until they all went back into the woods.

Alex got up to go inside to make something to go on the grill. She picked up the hamburgers and seasoned them, then she went to get the grill going.

Max had already started the grill. He was one step ahead of her.

How did you know that I was going to start cooking?

I heard you in the refrigerator. I figured that you were ready. I was going to get it ready anyways. I can put them on the grill. Go relax. We missed lunch so I will do dinner.

I can help. I am used to doing things so I have to be doing something.

Well what do you want to go with the hamburgers? Chips?

Yeah we can do that. We have a dip too. We have a cooler so whatever we do not use we can put everything that has to be cold in it.

Ok good. I thought I had seen it in the car.

Yes I had put some essentials in it. But they do not have to be cold. I usually always take something home that is cold in the cooler.

Well the burgers smell good. I will go in and grab the other stuff to go with them and the chips.

Ok I will make sure that they do not burn.

Ok. Be right back. Do you want a drink?

I will take a soda.

Ok I will get you one now and then bring out everything else.

Max went in and grabbed them both a soda and took out some of the things to go with the dinner. He brought them out to the table and gave Alex her drink. Then went back in to grab the rest of the stuff and brought it out and sat down at the table. Well this was a great time this weekend.

Yes it is. Always great to relax. No calls or anything, this is perfect.

Well Bill will take any emergency calls. I had told him that I did not want to be disturbed. I trust that he can handle things there.

Oh so it was you that made it so that we were not interrupted? How nice.

Yes it was. I know that we needed this time with no one interrupting our time away. This is how it should be. I need to check on the hamburgers and flip them over. I got cheese to put on them.

I love cheeseburgers. With all of the fixings. But we can get that this coming week when we go out for lunch or dinner.

Ah yes. I miss eating at our diner.

This is great though. Making food and cooking it on the grill. I love the outdoors. The summer is for being outside. It's too cold in the winter to be outside. But you know I know people that grill out all year long. They must do it in their garage.

Maybe. People in the further south like Florida can grill out all year long.

Yes my parents love it to be able to grill out all year long. They have friends over and have cook outs. They go to their neighbors' pool and cool off. But when it gets really hot they just stay inside where it is cool. You have to have an air conditioner there as it gets too hot there. The winter time it is still nice there. It was in the seventies yesterday. I have the weather app so I can check to see what the weather is going to be like.

I can see why more people go to Florida during the winters. I have friends up north who have parents that go to Florida each year. They have a trailer there in a senior park.

Max got up and put the cheese on the hamburgers as they were almost done. Oh, these look good. They have grill marks on them and everything. There is just something about a burger on the grill that makes them taste better.

Yes I agree Max. They do taste much better. And the weather has been perfect for our time here. No rain at all.

Well if it had rained then we would be inside finding something else to do. Like maybe playing cards.

If I had brought a deck of cards, replied Alex.

Oh but I did. We could have played strip poker.

Well I would have lost at that game because I do not play poker.

Oh well then guess who would have won. It would have been me. So let's play after dinner. I will teach you said Max

We will see. I want to be good at it so that you will be doing the stripping.

Well if you want to strip we can just do that without the game said Max. But I have a feeling that I have to behave while I am here.

Well maybe not. Let's just see how it goes. She already knew what she wanted. And she knew that she had to watch what she did because she did not want to mess things up with him. Her feelings for him were very strong. She has never felt this way for anyone before. She was happy that Max had feelings for her too. So she wanted to make sure that she did not move too fast and scare him away.

Max took the hamburgers off of the grill and let it burn out. He was happy with the way that they turned out.

Alex opened up the hamburger buns and put one on her plate as she got a hamburger and put it on the bun. Then she put some ketchup on and then picked it up to take a bite. It tasted so good. Great job Max. You did great cooking them..

You're welcome. Glad you liked it. I usually make them in a pan at home but I get the ones that are already made into patties.

That is what I do too because it is so much easier but I always add my own seasonings. I also like to buy the ones with the cheese already in them too.

Well, enjoy. They really did turn out good. I am glad that you liked them. Let's just enjoy our last day here. Tomorrow we have to head back and I really do not want to but I know that we have to be adults and go back to work. Max put a frown on his face and then smiled.

I know. But our clients need us to finish what we started. We have a court case coming up. And we are talking about work again. We have to stop this. We are on a short getaway.

Yes, let's just finish our dinner and I will clean up and you can sit here and relax.

I can help. I am not going to let you do it all.

Hey I said I will do it and I will. You just sit here and relax. I can do this myself. No arguing with me.

Ok. Alex had never had anyone wait on her before like this. She could not help but not want to do something. Besides, he had made a great meal. Then she remembered the chips. They forgot the chips. Oh well. This was enough as it was. They did not need anything else. Alex made herself another hamburger.

After dinner they both were full and Max had started to clean up the table and bring everything in. There really was not much to clean since they had cooked on the grill so there were no pans to wash. After Max finished washing everything up he let them dry in the dish drainer and went back out on the deck, sat down next to Alex. Would you like another drink?

No, I am fine thank you Max.

Ok I am going to get one in a bit. So if you want another one I can get you one when I get up again. I just want to enjoy this nice fresh air. It is cooling off here.

The locust started to sing in the trees. Alex loved to hear them. You know I used to pick the locust shells off the trees when I was a teen. Nothing like looking at them. I once saw one come out of the shell. Anything to do with nature I was into.

Wow that had to be cool. I was not into that kind of thing. I was too busy playing basketball and baseball with my friends.. My parents tried to keep me busy with sports. They wanted me out of the house outside doing what boys do.

Same with me. I was usually at my friends house and we would do things outside. Sometimes we ride our bikes to other friends house's. But my parents always knew where I was each time. I never went anywhere and did not tell them. Even back then there were kids that would come up missing. Thankfully none of them were anyone that I knew but one was at another school in the area. It is still sad to know that people would do that. The person was caught and is still in prison today. I believe that he got life.

That is sad. It is hard on the parents to lose a child to something like that. I could never imagine nor do I want to if I had lost a child like that.

I know. One of my friends was almost picked up by some guy but she ran away from him. I am glad that she got away from him. She was my best friend then. Now she moved away and I don't get to see her anymore.

I am sorry. I have lost many friends only because they are doing their own thing. I have one friend that I see sometimes but he has a family of his own now and the kids keep him busy.

Yeah that is what happened to me too. Everyone gets older and they have families they just do not have time for anything else as the kids keep them going.

Yes I am sure. It is good that the families are able to stay busy with sports and things. As long as the kids have something to do and it keeps them motivated. They do not get bored and stay on the computer all the time.

No just on their phones. So many kids are on their phones these days. I never had a phone of my own when I was younger. I was not into that kind of stuff. Most of my friends were close to where I lived so we just hung out together at my house or at the park.

As the night moved in, the mosquitoes came out. Well it is time to move inside. We are a meal for the mosquitoes. And I do not want to be eaten alive tonight, said Alex.

Well it is almost time for bed. Thank you Alex for a great day even though we just hung out here. It was nice just it being us.

Yes it was. We did not find any cute shops this time. Oh well but we did have fun doing a few other things like the concerts. Alex was tired and was ready to just call it a day. The next step was to work at getting Max moved in if he decided that was what he wanted to do.

Good night Alex. I will see you tomorrow.

Good night Max. See you then. Sleep well.

You to Alex. Max went into his room and shut the door. He really wanted to spend more time with Alex but he did not want to move too fast. They are learning more about each other outside of work. He was learning a whole different side of her. He also had to decide if he was going to move in with her but he would reside upstairs. It would be a lot better there where she is as it was quiet there and he could have more peace there. He would also have more time for himself.

CHAPTER FOURTEEN

Alex woke up first and went out to make a pot of coffee. She decided to go and take a shower while the coffee was brewing. She would let Max sleep in for a while so she tried to be quiet so as not to wake him up. After her shower she made herself a cup of coffee and went out on the deck to sit. She loved to sit outside and enjoy the animals. She checked out her phone to see what the weather was like and to send her mother a text that they would be driving home today. She always liked to keep in touch with her parents as much as she could since she was not able to talk to them as much due to her work schedule. And she did not want to spend time on the phone while she was with Max because she wanted her time with him alone.

Max woke up to the smell of coffee. Oh, someone is already up and made coffee. He put on his shorts and went out to the kitchen. He looked around for Alex then caught a glimpse of her out on the deck so he made a cup for himself and went out to sit with her.

Hello, how did you sleep? Max asked.

I slept well, replied Alex. She then looked up and noticed that he had no shirt on and the sight of his bare chest was what she liked to see. Well it sure is nice to see you with no shirt on. I can tell you do work out.

Yes I do. I can work out at home some but I take time to go to the gym.

Alex did not know what to think about the women looking at him while he worked out. She felt a little jealous. She figured he must get hit on by other women. But she needed to not get like that. He liked her and she definitely liked him. She has just been afraid to show it before. But now he made her partner and put her in charge of going through applicants once they started to come in. She would have to put in an ad in the paper for new potential employees and then get a background check on each one. This is an important part for her and she had to do a good job at finding good people to help run the office. She also had to check out social media and to find out all of the information that she could find on each one.

So what do you want to do about breakfast? Asked Max.

Not really sure. I picked up some muffins. Do you want something to eat as I will make you breakfast?

It's up to you, said Max.

What do you want? I can make us some eggs and have the muffins.

That sounds good, said Max.

Alex got up and went inside to make the eggs with cheese. She made sure that she used up the rest of the eggs and also she poured milk into a glass for each of them to finish that up as well.

Thank you Alex. This is great. They both sat at the table and ate in silence. Alex had a lot on her mind for this coming week. She was happy that Max had trusted her enough to make the right choices when finding good candidates for the job. They definitely needed the help. Hiring Bill and Madison was just a start. Madison would be able to print out the applications that come in and put them in Alex's box for her to pick up and go over.

We will have to talk to a contractor about adding on to the building or we will have to find a warehouse. But with a warehouse we will be able to have more people working with us. We work together as a team. We are not looking for detectives, we are looking for a team as we work together on each thing. Each person will specialize in certain details of the job. It will make the cases flow through easier as long as each person does their job correctly.

So would it be better to look for a warehouse. It would be easier for you as you do not have to hire someone and wait for it to be done. How many people do you want to hire? We only have three extra offices. And mine is not big enough to make it for two people. I think that looking for a warehouse would be much better. That way we can hire the right amount of people to be on. And Madison will have a key to let the others in if we decide to take time off.

You're right there. I think that just looking for a warehouse would be much easier. Then if we are not able to find one that is reasonable then we might just look into adding on our own office. I would just sell our office space for the warehouse. And take out a loan for the rest.

Well this week we will look for a warehouse. That way we do not have to wait for construction to be done. And the warehouse does not have to be perfect. As long as we have room for all of the desk units to be put up.

After Breakfast Alex got up and washed up the dishes and got them put away. They finished drinking the coffee out on the deck and just enjoyed watching the squirrels running around in the trees. Alex hated to have to end the trip. She enjoyed being with someone and having a good time with.

Well that was a great breakfast Alex. Thank you. This week is going to be a very busy week as I will be sorting through my stuff and packing up and getting ready for the move. How much do you want for the room plus half of everything? How much do you think?

I think six hundred for everything would be sufficient. What do you think?

That is a great price. I pay eight hundred for the apartment I have right now and it is a one bedroom plus utilities.

Ok great. You can start moving in anytime.

I hope to start by next weekend. I don't really have a lot of stuff so this will be a great move.

Having Max move in would be great because that way she won't be alone especially at night and it would be great to have someone to cook for besides herself. With Max being upstairs it would be a comfort and he could have his privacy at any time.

They were on their way home and decided to stop off at a truck stop for lunch. They had a buffett there which is better as they could fill up on everything. One thing that they both loved to do.

Wow, I am glad that we found this place. And it smells good from the outside. Hope that the food tastes good inside.

I hope so too, said Alex. If it is, we can put this place on the list of places to come back to if we decide to go back to the campground again. There are still many places that we can go to.

Max opened the door and Alex walked in. Thank you Max.

Inside they saw a place for the Truckers to be able to rest while they were stopped. They were also able to get a hot shower and wash their clothes. The restaurant provided a hot homemade style buffet for them to get a like home cooked meal. There was also a store for them to shop for personal items such as clothing and other items that they might need while they are on the road.

Max and Alex went into the Restaurant and were seated by the hostess. They put in their drink order and told her that they wanted the buffet. Most of the truckers were sitting alone and there was an area for them to also sit and watch TV. It was more of a comfort place for them to relax and eat. Here they all got to talk together if they wanted to.

Oh this looks good said Max. Now if we were on the road we could go to many places like this.

Well there is a place like this close to us. I dont go there much because we usually go to the diner. But we can go there for dinner, it's a bit out of our way when you move in but I don't mind. Plus we can take one car then too and save on gas.

That is right. Max looked over the assortment of meats, vegetables and breads then went to check out the desserts. Ok you start where you want, I am going to start here.

Ok but you still should eat dinner too. You can't just eat dessert only.

Says who? I don't see my mother here do you?

No. Ok do what you want to do but when you complain of a stomach ache don't blame me on that one.

Max laughed, I am going to get some food but I really want to go ahead and grab my dessert first while it's here.

Oh but the pasta and salad bar is just over there.

What? There is more food? Max had to go check out the other two bars as well. We hit the jackpot here.

I feel that they will have to close as they run out of food with you. Max loved to eat and did not gain any weight. Alex really did not know where he put it all.

Alex got a few things on her plate and went and sat down. Max's apple pie was sitting on the table. She will go up and get dessert after she gets done eating. She wanted to get some ice cream so if she got it now it would be melted before she ate it. Unless…. If she ate it before her meal. But she knew that she could not do that.

Wow Alex, look at this. There is such a selection here. We might be here for a few hours. I love this.I have not been to a place like this in a long time.

Well that is good that you like it here. Alex took a bite of her Turkey with gravy and could not believe how great it tasted. She was impressed. Wow this is really home made food here. It's amazing. She tried the mashed potatoes and found that they were real and not the instant kind. Oh wow I am in love.

Yes, this pot roast is good too. But not as good as yours of course. He knew that he had to say that as he was going to be eating more of her cooking and she was a great cook. The pot roast was close to hers. He had also got mashed potatoes as well as macaroni and cheese. He wanted to go back for some pasta after but he had to eat his pie while he had room for it. Remember dessert is the most important meal of the day.

Alex finished what she had and went back up for more food. This time she did get some pot roast. It was so tender. She got some more mashed potatoes and gravy as well as some stuffing. She also got a scoop of carrots to go with her meal.

Wow, you're going to like the pot roast. Said Max. But like I said yours is better, it has more flavor. I like the way you season yours.

Alex tried it and agreed that it was good but hers tasted better. I guess that they do not season it as much because not everyone can have a lot of salt or even pepper. Alex did season it with the salt and pepper but it was still missing her other seasonings that she put in hers but it did taste better. The gravy helped as well. The stuffing was amazing. After she finally got done eating she was ready for some ice cream.

Max went back up for some more food as well. He had filled his plate earlier and had more than what Alex had. But he wanted some more of what he had missed before. And he had also got some ice cream. Even though he ate quite a bit now he was set for the rest of the day. He did not want to fix anything later after he got home.

Max and Alex finally made it back home and they unloaded the car. Max helped Alex bring everything into the house. He was a great help unloading the car for her. Alex started the laundry so it would be less for her to do during the week. She really wanted to get it started that night while she caught up on her shows. She was very tired but she was not ready to go to bed yet.

Thank you again Alex. I had a great time.

You're welcome. Did you want to go home tonight or wait till tomorrow? There is a spare room upstairs where you can sleep tonight.

No, I need to get home and unload my car. Plus my work clothes are there. I will see you tomorrow. Thanks for the offer though. I will be here soon enough. Besides, I do not want you to get tired of me so soon.

That will never happen. Alex smiled.

Have you ever had a roommate before?

Only in college. I only had a few roommates that I liked and got along with. But I had several friends that I had in college and loved and still keep in touch with a few.

Ok well I am going to go. I will see you in the morning. I will pick up the coffee tomorrow. Max went over to Alex and gave her a hug and a kiss on the cheek. Thanks again for everything.

Your welcome Max. Anytime. It's great having you along. We have fun together.

Lock your door as he walks out to the car.

I will always do even though I live out here. Get home safely. Text me when you get home.

I will, replied Max. He got in his car and made his way out of the driveway.

Alex shut the door and turned off her porch light and locked the door. She went in and sat down on the couch and felt loneliness since Max is gone now. Max had texted her a half an hour later and she knew that she could go ahead and get ready for bed.She put the clothes in the dryer and then went to bed.

CHAPTER FIFTEEN

Alex got to work first. She went in and called the newspaper company and put an ad in for more Detectives. They were able to either apply online or they could come in and fill out an application.

Madison showed up next. Alex went out to tell her that there would be applications coming in for the Detective jobs and that she would take them as they came in.

Ok, replied Madison. I will keep watch for them and will put them in your mailbox or put them on your desk if your door is open.

Thank you, replied Alex. I am taking over the applicants. We will also be looking for a warehouse as this is not big enough for all of the new people coming in. We need more work space.

Oh wow that sounds interesting. I think that there is one for rent down the road.

We will have to check that out later, replied Alex. Hopefully it will be a good fit for us.

I hope so too. Since you're going to expand.

Yes for sure.

The door opened and Max walked in with Coffee.

Oh Coffee is here. I need some. I did not sleep well last night. Too much on my mind.

Here you go, replied Max, handing Alex one and then Madison. Is Bill here yet?

I have not seen him. Replied Alex. I was here first.

Ok well as soon as he comes in will you let me know. We need to have a meeting this morning. And I have to send everything over to the Judge so that he will have it for the trial. Hopefully that will be this week. So we can get this case closed and put the three men in prison. I hope that the Jury finds them Guilty.

Yes, me too. Alex was wanting to get this done as soon as possible. There was no bail set for either one of them. For what they have done there would not be a bail set for them anyways. She was glad of that.

Ok so if you want to go ahead and start with those applications if any comes in I will be in my office busy sending the Judge what he needs. After Bill comes in we need to have a meeting.

Alright. Oh there might be a warehouse available down the road from us. Perfect location. So I can find out who owns it and I can get a hold of them.

Ok sure that would be great. Please call them and make an appointment for us to look at it. Hopefully tomorrow.

Ok sure I can do that Max.

Alex went out the door to go and check out the warehouse to find out who to call to rent it. Hopefully it was not too much monthly and that it was not already rented out. As she got closer to the building a car pulled up in front of it. A tall man got out in a suit and walked up to the door.

Excuse me sir, are you the owner of this building?

Why yes I am. Can I help you?

Yes, have you rented this yet?

No I haven't. Are you interested?

Yes, my partner and I are. We are looking for a bigger place.

And what do you do?

I am a Detective. We are looking for a bigger place as we are getting more people to work for us. Our office is right up the road here. We just need more space.

Well I can show you around now. Or what about tomorrow?

Can I look at it now? I can call my partner to come down now.

Sure you can look now.

What are you asking for to rent it?

Well I am hoping to sell it eventually but for now I can rent it.

What do you want for it?

Eighty-five thousand. You said you have a smaller building. Do you rent it or own it?

My partner owns it.

I am actually looking for a smaller building. This one was too big.

Ok well let me call my partner and have him come down now. He can walk down.

Ok sure that would be great.

Alex called Max and he decided to come right down to look at the warehouse.

Max came walking down towards the building, Alex was waiting outside for him.

What is this? Is it a warehouse?

Yes and it is the size that we need. We just have to look inside to see what shape it is in.

Ok great, well let's go in. Max did not have much time to decide since he was busy with the report that he had to send to the Judge.

We have to see it today as he has someone else coming to look at it.

They always say that they have someone else to look at it so that you will make an offer

Yeah but we never know. I don't think that it has even hit the realtor yet.

Still though I am not sure.

Well let's check it out and see.

How much is he asking for it?

Eighty-five thousand, replied Alex. Let's go and see what we think.

Max and Alex both walked into the front door. What they saw amazed them.

Wow this really is some place. It was big enough for everything that they needed and the building went back quite a ways.

It really is worth the money as I am not asking a lot for it. I need to sell it so that I can find something else to put my business into. This was much bigger than I needed. Since most of my associates have left I really do not need anything this big. Before it was perfect as I had the associates here that I needed to work for me.

Well please show us around.

Ok well the front part is the reception areas, I had several as we had many associates. And back in the other part was the offices, there is also a big conference room there.

Is there an upstairs? It looks like there is one.

Yes there is an upstairs.Let me show you the upstairs.

Ok thank you. Then I have to get back to my office.

Sure that's fine. I will get with you to look at your building.

Yeah that will be great. We could trade and I will pay you the difference, replied Max.

Oh that would be great for me. I would not have to wait until I sell this. How much are you asking for your building?

Forty Thousand. It was either I find a bigger place or I would have to add on to our building.

So is this something that you're looking for?

Yes it is. Can I talk with you later about it? Do you have a number I can call you at?

Sure, here is my card, replied Mr. Bryant. My first name is Tayler.

Hello. My name is Max Lee and this is my partner Alex Tibbles.

I like the name Tibbles. Very unique.

Thank you, replied Alex. We really have to go but we will be in touch this afternoon.

Great, Thank you, replied Mr Bryant.

Alex and Max left to go back to the office.

They both walked into the office and Madison gave them a message. It's from the Judge. He is waiting on the report.

Ok I will send it to him as soon as I can. I need to get it right in. I was almost done but had to look at the building. Is Bill here yet?

Yes he is in his office.

Ok thank you. I will talk to him after. I have to get that report in.

Ok Max, I will be in my office until you get ready to do the meeting.

Ok thanks. I have to get this done. So you are going to have to take any calls that come in. Max then walked into his office and closed the door.

Alex went into her office and checked out warehouses online. There were a few in the area but not as big as the one that she had looked at. She had also checked out the price of them and they were more than the one that they had looked at. She looked at the pictures of the ones available online. One was really nice but it was too much money. They did not need anything nice really as they were just going to be working there. She looked into a few outside of the area and they were more expensive so this one was the best one.

Bill came out of the office and knocked on Max's door. Alex called him into her office and explained to him that Max was working on the case for the Judge and that he had to get it out right away.

After Max gets done there will be a meeting so it should be soon.

Ok thanks. I am going to look at the old cases. I have one that I have been working on.and I think I might have a lead on it. The person of interest is in prison already but I think this might be connected with this one as well. I just have to find proof.

Oh that would be great if it is. Then we can close the case if it is solved.

Yes I agree. It would be amazing if we could solve this one for the parents.. They were really close to their daughter.

Yes I see that. So sad that she died a horrible death. All of the cold cases are hard to read about the victims. I am checking in to see how many of them are linked to the same person.

I agree I have wondered that myself but we have to get through them. But first we have to close this case and we can work on the Cold cases when we can. We just came to a dead end and I feel bad for the families because I do not want to just leave them. So this is why we have to get a bigger team to get these closed up. We have to find out who did this. Their killers are still out there.

So have you placed an ad in for the jobs yet?

Yes I placed one today so I think that it will go out tomorrow. So Madison will be taking the applications and printing off the ones online so I can start interviewing people hopefully soon.

That will be good because it is important that we get some good people in here. I hope that they are going to work out. So many people out there want to work but are not able to find a good job. So they end up working at jobs that they do not like.

That is why I hope that we can get people in here that know what they are doing. I am not able to train people to do this. They have to have taken college classes to do what we do.

Well that is why I would only accept the applications of those that have been in college for this. Or those with experience.

Yes that is why Max chose you to work with us.

Well ok now that I am done we can do the meeting. Everyone in my office. Max was ready to share the news that he had been wanting to do in the morning but he got held up and now he could make his announcement.

What is up? askedBill.

Well over the weekend I had been doing a lot of thinking. I know we had gone away to relax but I just can not do that. I just kept thinking about what we had to do next. That we have to grow as a team. So I have put Alex in charge of HR and working with me as well and Bill you're going to be in charge of the Cold cases but your main purpose is investigating the cases. Alex and I will be doing the reports of the case and the autopsies. You will be doing the investigations at the crime scene and working with the family.

Ok that sounds good. I can do that.

And for the big news we are looking at Warehouses to maybe move into. We need something bigger than what we have or we will have to add on here. I looked at one Warehouse just down the street. It is big enough for what I want it for.

That is great, replied Bill. So are you going to sell this?

Only if I find a place that we can move into.Which I think that we have, he wants a smaller place like ours. Said Max. So I am thinking about taking the offer.

Wonderful news. So why are we looking for another building?

Well we might not be. But I kinda want to see what else there is out there.

I have looked up Warehouses for sale or rent and they really were not what we were looking for Max, replied Alex.

I knew that there was a reason why I kept you around, smiled Max.

Well I thought it was because you liked my good looks.

Ok you two do I need to get the hose? Asked Madison.

Yes you just might have to. This guy is on fire. Said Alex.

Ok well Bill I want you for now to work on the cold cases. I think that we have this case wrapped up. We will not be able to hear back from the Judge until maybe tomorrow. I will be surprised if we hear back by the end of the day. He really wants to get this case closed. They are already bringing in the Jurors. Alex, did you put the ad in the paper for possible candidates for Detectives?

Yes I did. It will be in the paper tomorrow but it should be posted online today.

Awesome thank you. I knew I could count on you. You are always on top of everything.

That is the way to do things that is all. You give me something to do and I get right on it.

And that is why I made you my partner.

Yes I agree, replied Bill. You really do come through for us here. I know that I have not been here much but Max talks about you all the time when we talk.

Oh he does huh. Well that is nice to know, said Alex.

Well you are a great partner and I do tell others about that. So what do you want to do for lunch? Then we can go and talk to Mr Byrant about the building.

It is up to you. Wherever you want to go to Max. We can hopefully celebrate.

Yes, ok let's all go to Steak and Ale today.

Oh yes lets go, shouted Madison. Bill and I can ride together and meet you there so you and Alex can go to the Warehouse after.

It's only down the street so we can all go together. Replied Alex.

Sure that is fine, said Madison. Let's go.

At the restaurant it was starting to get busy for the lunch rush. A hostess came over to seat them. We have a nice booth over here.

Thank you, replied Max. And it is all on one bill.

Ok, that is fine. Your waitress will be over shortly. Here are the menus. We have a two for one steak dinner special today.

Oh that sounds good. But I still want to look at the menu. There are so many choices here.

Yes there is, replied Alex. If you want to do the two for one dinner I will do that too with you.

No pick what you want. We deserve this. You're an amazing worker, you all are. I am so glad that I have picked all of you as you have shown your worth to me.

Alex looked at the menu. Still wanted the two for one meal.

The waitress came over to take their drink order and went through the specials.

They all ordered soda and then put in a few appetizers.

So when I get back I want to go over the one case that I was working on, replied Bill. There are two victims that were murdered the same way and I think that they were connected with the one case that was solved. I think that the man in prison, also killed before. But he was stupid and got caught during the second murder.

I want to go over that case with you to see if it could be. I hope so.

The waitress came over with the drinks. Your appetizer will be out shortly. Can I get you anything else?

Steak sauce if you have it.

We have our very own in house steak sauce that comes with your meal.

Oh thank you. This is really an amazing place here. I like it.

Well thank you. Yes the owner took it over a few years ago and he left everything the way it was. The customers have appreciated the way it was kept since the changeover. She then left and went back to take care of other orders while theirs was being done.

So hopefully we can do the deal by switching out both buildings but I will owe more so I will have to go to the bank to take out a loan.

I will go with you since we are partners. I can go in on the loan as well. That way it will not be just you having to pay it all back. I can do my part too.

I would not expect you to do that. I should be able to have it paid back within a few years.

Well we can talk about that later. Said Alex.

Ok.

The appetizers came out and everyone was hungry and ready to dig into them. Buffalo wings were a great way to start a meal.

Oh, these are good. Not too hot but just right.

I agree. These are really good. Might be the best wings yet, replied Bill. I never had these before. I usually always get the potato skins. They are amazing. They come with sour cream.

Oh I saw those too and I wish you had said something we could have ordered them too.

Next time my friend, replied Bill. Right now I just want to eat these. They are really great.

Before they were done the waitress came out with their food. Here you go. Enjoy. If there is anything else that I can get you please let me know.

Can we get an order of Potato skins with extra sour cream? Asked Max.

You sure can. Anything else?

A refill on our drinks please.

Sure coming right up.

Why did you order the potato skins? We hardly have enough room to eat our dinner.

Speak for yourself, replied Bill. I could eat two of these dinners.

Oh wow. I will have one or two.

You're going to want more. They are amazing. We really should have just gotten the appetizers for our meal said Bill.

Well I will have to take the rest of my dinner home for tonight then. Because I will be full before I get to eat my lunch.

This is a day of celebration. To our growing team.

They all raised their glasses and clanked them and cheered.

Max started eating his steak and melted. Oh this is so good.

Yes it is, Alex replied. I am glad that we got the two for one dinner.

Well I wanted to go ahead and try it and it is amazing. Not that it's any better than yours, nothing is better than having it outside on the grill. He knew that he had to save himself otherwise Alex might not cook for him again. He does not want to get into the dog house before he moves in.

Wow this is really good, I am glad that you like it. Alex was enjoying her dinner as well. She had to season it a little bit more.

After dinner they all went to the Warehouse. Mr. Bryant was still there. Max parked the car and they all got out to look around inside. Mr Bryant was in the back when they came in and he came out. He was surprised that Max was back there already.

Well hello, I did not expect you back so soon.

Yes these are my other two co workers and I wanted them to see the Warehouse too. This is definitely going to work for us. Do you want to go and look at our building?

Sure I can go look at it. But let your coworkers look around and then we can go to yours.

Ok. Thanks.

Mr Bryant gave them a tour around the building.

At the Office, Mr Bryant came down to look at the office building.

Well this is actually something that I had in mind. I think that I can make it work with my other employees. I like that it has a kitchen break room area.

Yes it works really well for us. Even though Alex and I go out to eat when we are out working.

Well it would work better for me as I usually work inside of the office. The only time that I go out is if I am meeting clients.

What do you do?

I am a Lawyer.

Oh well that is nice to know and nice to meet you.

Thank you. I will think about this and I will get back to you. If you're interested in my building, here is my real estate person and her number. Just give her a call.

Ok thank you. Much appreciated, said Max.

Your welcome and thank you, said Mr. Bryant. He then left to go back to the warehouse.

Well he is a nice guy or at least he seems to be a nice guy. And the building is what we need. I will give the real estate person a call. The other places that Alex had looked online at were not what we had wanted.

Yes some were in rough shape. Only one seemed in better condition but they wanted more for it and it looked smaller than what we had gone to look at.

Well let's go and see what we have here and I want to check out that case that Bill had looked at.

Ok sure.

Madison checked the answering machine, no new messages. She then looked at her emails and nothing new there either so there were no new applications. She was hoping that there would be a few there.

Bill went into his office and got the file that he was looking at and went to Max's office and showed him the file. This is the file that I had found, I need to open it up and check out what other evidence is there. Do we have anything here for evidence?

No it is all down at the police station in the evidence room. You will have to go there to see what they have if anything is stored there. Some cases really do not have much there for clues.

Ok I will call and see if they have anything. She was killed and found in the field near the school where she went and lived close by. The way that she was killed is similar to the one case that was closed last year that you had. I went through the cases because I had read this case and it seemed familiar to this case. And if I am right then the guy is already locked up. But we will have to prove that he did this girl too.

So he did not own up to this one. How did we miss this?

You just did not put two and two together. But it was only you and Alex so you really did not have any help with this. Now you do. This is my thing. I have solved many cold cases. This is what I like to do. It helps the families to find peace to know that their family member's killer is locked up.

Thank you Bill. Go and find out what you can. Then we can open the case back up and get it closed.

Will do, replied Bill. I want to get this done for the family.

At the end of the day Alex was ready to go home. She needed to get some things done as she was busy over the weekend. She also needed some rest. Even though you go and rest on vacation you need a vacation from the vacation.

Well, let's go home. I am going to go and start going through my things so that I can get packed up and get the apartment cleaned out of what I no longer need.

Ok well I will see you tomorrow. You can start bringing stuff over at any time. Here is a key for you.

Ok thanks. I will start in a few days. I just have to go through things and take up to the Salvation army or to a thrift store.

Well, bring what you want to my house. We can find a place for it. You do not have to give it away. Keep it.

Ok I will bring some stuff over and if we are not able to find a place for it I can take it to the thrift store then.

Sure that's fine. I am sure we can find someplace for all of your stuff. Besides you have a couple of rooms upstairs.

That is true. Ok I will start packing tonight and get it done all week. So hopefully by next week I can get moved in.

I can come over tomorrow and help you if you want. I don't think that we will be that busy tomorrow. Unless I get some applications then maybe.

That is true. I will have to get a hold of the lady this week to talk about the warehouse. Just to get in there and make a bid. I am going to go ahead and put in for the full price just in case. Then sell my building as well.

Maybe we can get the same lady to look at your building.

That would be a great idea. She knows more about what to do. And since she is selling that building it is close to ours so why not.

Well anyways let's go home. I have things to do and to clean the upstairs so you can move in. I have to vacuum up there. It has been awhile since I have done it since it is not being used. See you tomorrow.

Ok sure. See you then. Have a great night.

Alex got home and put her lunch in the microwave and heated it up. She then grabbed the milk out and poured herself a glass. Once her dinner was heated up she ate it before having to go upstairs to clean. She was happy that he was moving in but then she was afraid that she might be making a mistake. She had hoped that everything would go well. She had planned on making the spare bedroom into another room for him if he needed it. Letting him have his own space would be great and she hardly ever had anyone come over to spend the night anyways so why keep the spare room as that. She could just turn it into another room for him. The bed was a full size bed. She wondered what size bed he had. She was sure that he had a full size bed too. She would have to see what he had to bring over.

After she got done cleaning and had done up another load of laundry she called it a day and went to bed. She turned on the TV to watch a movie, but she did not make it all the way through as she had fallen asleep before it finished. It was going to be a busy week.

CHAPTER SIXTEEN

Alex woke up and it was a beautiful Sunny day out. She got up and got her shower. She could not wait to have Max move in. She was excited but still nervous all at the same time. It had been awhile since she had lived with a guy since her fiance had left her. They talked about getting married until he got cold feet. She got dressed, grabbed a piece of toast and went out the door to work. She went to the coffee place and grabbed four cups of coffee and went to work.

At work Max was already there. She brought him his cup of coffee and left Madison her cup on her desk. Bill was not there yet. So she put his coffee on his desk. He could heat it up in the microwave when he came in.

So I got to thinking Max, I don't use the spare room upstairs so you can use that room too. I mean I have friends over once in a while but they can sleep in my room if they come over. It's not a big deal and it's not often so you can use that room too. What size bed do you have?

I have a full size bed. Why?

The bed that is upstairs is practically new. I don't know if you want to use that one or your bed. Either way it's ok. I can put it out in storage.

No, I am sure that you can just keep it as a spare room.

Also since we are going in together to get the warehouse you don't have to pay the six-hundred. I will just do three-hundred. That way it will be easier for you.

No, I can do the six-hundred.

Well we will see what we will have to do for the loan for the Warehouse.

Madison came in. Hello to you both. Thank you for the coffee.

You're welcome Madison.

You're really nice to bring me coffee.

I brought it for everyone. That is just me. Let me know when some applications come in.

I will. I will check the emails here and I have printed off some applications if anyone comes in for one.

Ok great. I want to start interviewing people soon. So that we can get the team together.

How is the case going?

Good but we are waiting for the Trial. All three are in Jail so we are waiting for the trial to come though. Hopefully it will be soon. We just have to wait and hear from the judge.

Ok well I will let you know as soon as he calls.

It will be this week. But we have to go to the bank to take out a loan for the warehouse. Once we put in an offer for it with the realtor.

Alex went into her office and sat down. She wanted to check out the new prospects as soon as they came in to do background checks and to find out if they have been in trouble before. Some people have done time when they were younger and have made their way to turning their life around.

Madison came in with one application. I did have one once I got into the emails. So here you go.

Ok Thank you Madison. I will look it over.

Alex took the application, she did a background check on him and also looked him up on social media. But there were a few other people with the same name so she would have to look a little better. Since she did not know what he looked like she had to make sure that she was looking for the right person. She will have to call him in for an interview. So far the background check and he was good. No prior so he was hireable. She would have to check to see just how experienced he is. She gave him a call to see if he could come in that day.

Max came in and wanted to go to the bank to see if he could get a bank loan for the Warehouse. There was no reason why he would not qualify. He had called the realtor and she said that she would talk to him about the offer but he wanted to go and see how much he could get for the loan. He did not want to get his hopes up and then not get the loan. Can you go with me to go for the loan?

I have an interview coming in soon. Can we wait until after.

Sure we can wait till then. Why don't we wait until after lunch. I am not sure how long this is going to take.

Usually it is an hour or so to try to get a loan. It's a business loan so we should be able to get it and we are both going to apply for it. I will be the co-applicant.

Ok, sounds good replied Max. Let me know how the interview goes.

I will. But I will interview everyone but I am not going to hire yet. How many people do you want to hire?

Let's start out with eight.

Ok. I have one so we can see how many more come in.

The door opened and in came a young man. I am here about the job.

Sure, here is an application. You can have a seat over there and fill it out.

Thank you, My name is Rick.

Well hello Rick. Nice to meet you.

Is the manager here today? Asked Rick.

She is but we are accepting applications. She will go over your application and then give you a call.

Can I please talk to her today? I really need a job.

Do you have experience in Detective work?

Yes I do. I was working in Florida and had to move back here to help take care of my parents.

Do you understand that the hours could be at any time and long?

Yes I do. My parents are doing better now and my sister lives with them now too.

Ok because we need someone that can work the long hours.

Alex had heard him come in and the both talking. She went out to talk to him. Hi Rick. When you're done I will be glad to go over your application. I am not hiring anyone today, I am just doing interviews.

Ok sure, replied Rick. Thank you.

The door opened again. It was Alex's interview.

Can I help you? asked Madison.

Yes I have an appointment with Alex.

Sure I will go and get her.

Ok thank you.

Madison went into Alex's office and told her that her interview was there.

Ok please send him in.

You can go back, said Madison.

Ok thank you. The young gentleman got up to go back to the office.

Madison went back to checking other emails while Alex was back in her office. Then Max came out of his office and headed to Madison's desk. Can you please file these.

Sure.

Is the interview person here yet?

Yes and she has another one right after.

Ok good. I just want to get this loan thing out of the way.

Yeah I agree. Then you know what you can do from there.

Yes. We really need to move into something bigger. That is the reason for the loan. Ok well when she gets done please let me know.

I sure will, replied Madison.

Max went back into his office and shut the door. He was hoping to hear something from the judge today. Nothing. Hopefully he will call tomorrow. He wanted to get this case closed. It is not like that he did not know about the case before so why is he waiting now to get it done.

After the two interviews were over Alex and Max went out for lunch before going to the Bank.

So how did the interviews go?

One is good, the other not so well. But I have to do a background check on the second one. Hopefully I have more applicants come in.

I hope so too. We really need the help. We have to get those other cases done now that Bill is on the case. We need more people to check them out.

Yes I agree but we have to make sure that they know what they are doing. Where do you want to go to eat?

Let's go to the diner. Replied Alex.

Ok sure we can go there.

They both got into Max's car and went to the diner.

Inside it was a little busy.

The hostess came over to seat them and handed them two menus.

Your waitress will be right over.

Ok thank you.

The specials were roasted turkey and mashed potatoes with gravy with a side order of carrots.

Oh this looks good said Max. I am going to get that. Their food is always good and I have had that once before and it was really good.

I think I am going to order the same thing, Alex replied. I was thinking about the spaghetti but the special really does sound good.

Well at least we like the same things.

Yes we do. Which is great.

The waitress came over and took their drink order as well as their lunch order.

Ok coming up.

So have you heard from the judge yet or the realtor?

No on both. I wish that the Judge would call me to let me know when the date was going to be. I really hope that it is this week. Today I hope that I can leave early so I can go home and start packing more stuff. I found that I have stuff to actually get rid of like clothes that do not fit me anymore. Since I have been working out I am more buff now.

Alex saw his buff at the campground and she liked what she saw. Oh well that is good, she replied. She could not let him know that she had noticed. She was happy to see the new him. But she did not care if he was working out or not because either way he was still hot. She had to keep her cool about herself. Now he would be even closer with her and she had to learn to keep herself together and not try to attack him like a bear going after its prey.

The waitress came back with their drinks. The food will be out soon. It has been popular today. We are almost out.

Thank you. Glad we made it in before it was all gone, replied Max.

Can I get you anything else?

No, I think we are good for now.

Ok She walked out back.

I have been hungry since ten this morning, said Max. I did not get to eat this morning. I was running late.

If I had known I would have picked you up something to eat.

No, it's ok. I had some peanuts that I had in my office.

That is not breakfast.

I know but it is better than nothing. And you were only supposed to have one interview that turned into two.

Well I would not have had two if he was able to come back. But I still have to check him out so I might have to do another one. Depending on how his background check goes.

The waitress came back out with their food.

Oh that smells so good and looks even better.

Thank you. It really is good. I tried some earlier.

Alex and Max both ate quietly as they knew that they had to get to the bank soon. He still had a lot to do at home.

At the bank Max and Alex sat and filled out paperwork for the loan that they were approved for. Max was happy that everything was moving forward as planned. Now he just had to get a hold of the realtor with the money. They both would be able to pay the loan back in fifteen years and both knew that they were not going anywhere. Max had trusted her so much with this next step. It was about time that things were finally starting to come together now.

Well this is not as bad as I thought it was going to be, said Alex. Good thing that we have good credit.

Yes it is. I never buy anything that I am not able to afford. I make goals, and this is the next goal that I have to go for. And with your help you made it happen.

Did you make me a partner so that I would help you out? Asked Alex.

No, not at all. But since we are going to be partners I want it in both of our names. You deserve this. You have worked so hard to get where you are now. You are an amazing person and I love that about you. You know what you want and you go for it.

Well, so do you. You have come through so much and have done well. You took any problem and worked it out.

Back at the office Madison had handed Alex some more applications.

Oh wow thank you. This is great. I will get to work on this now.

I will be leaving shortly to go home and get things done since there really is not much to do.

Ok I will see you tomorrow then, replied Alex.

Everyone else can go too. There really is not much left to do since this case is almost done. Alex you can work on the applications tomorrow.

Sure ok. So I will see you tomorrow then. I will go through them tomorrow and maybe more will come in as well.

I am sure that there will be more in the morning.

Ok well I will see you all in the morning. Alex locked up and headed for home. She had to get things done at home.

At home Alex fixed herself some dinner before getting at the things that needed to be done. She did not want to have to clean while Max was moving in. She wanted to make sure that the house was in order before he moved in. She still had to clean the bathroom upstairs. Even though she did not use the bathroom upstairs she still had to clean some things. Then she would clean the downstairs. She turned on some music and started to work while listening. She then started to dance to the music. Korean music was so amazing. She did not understand what they were saying but she loved the beat of the music. No matter what you are, music is universal. Alex had started to listen to Korean music since Max is Korean and she has been learning more about the culture and anything else that is to know about it. Make it right came on the radio and Alex had to stop and sing along. Alex got the laundry all done and put away and did the dishes. She dusted everything and so far everything is done. It was late in the night and she knew that she had to go to bed. She felt relaxed knowing that she did not have anything left to do to prepare for Max moving in.

CHAPTER SEVENTEEN

By the time Alex got to work Max was already there. Alex brought in breakfast for the both of them. She was too tired to make breakfast this morning and she knew that she had the applications to go through.

Hi Max. I brought you breakfast. I am going to work on those applications from yesterday. If there are any more then I will work on those as well today.

Thank you Alex. I got a lot done yesterday. I hope to get some stuff moved in tomorrow.

Ok that will be fine. You have the key. I can come over tomorrow and help you move some stuff over then as well for you.

Ok that will be good. Then on the weekend I will have a few of my friends to come and help me move over the big stuff.

Sure that will be fine. I should be home all day but if I am not you have your own key. I may have to go and get groceries.

Ok or we can both go. It's up to you.

Sure. Well I am going to go work now on those applications.

Ok. Good luck.

Thank you. Alex then turned and went into her office and shut the door. She went through all of the applications, there were a total of seven so far plus the two that came in yesterday. She ran them all through the background check. They all came back great. No one had a record. So they should be good for hire. She just has to check to see what kind of experience that they have and schooling. Some have been to college for Criminal Justice so they will be the first to call. The others are going to go in another folder. They did not have the time to train anyone that did not have schooling for the job. So those that made it this far she checked to see if they have social media. Only a few did and they seemed to be doing well. So she made the decision to start making appointments for the afternoon interviews. Four had made it to the good pile. She gave all four a call and three could come in that afternoon.

Alex walked out to see Madison. She had a few more applications come in. Alex would go through them as well and see if any of them qualify for the job. There were a few more with no experience even though the ad said MUST HAVE EXPERIENCE! So she just put them in the pile of not qualified. She went through the background checks and gave them a call. They will be coming in tomorrow for interviews in the morning. She did not want to make it for that afternoon as she did not know how long each one was going to be.

It was getting towards lunch time and Alex's first interview was at one so she decided to go and see if Max wanted lunch.She got up to go into his office and he was not there. She went to the front to where Madison was. Have you seen Max?

Yes he is at the courthouse to talk to the Judge. He had some things to go over with the paperwork.

Oh ok. Well I am just going to order lunch then and have it delivered. I have interviews today starting at one.

Oh yes, here are some more applications. Where are you going to order from?

I am going to order a salad. Do you want anything?

Sure I will get one too. Do you want me to call it in? And from where?

Yes I want to order from the Diner down the road, A chicken Salad, same for Max and get whatever you want. Is Bill still here?

No, he left for lunch.

Oh ok. So I will give you some money, Find out how much it is and then just give them the rest as a tip. I will get yours too.

Well thank you Alex. That is sweet of you.

No Problem Madison. My pleasure. And we work together so that is what we do. Well until we get more people hired anyway. We can still go out as a small group.

Alex went back into her office and got the money for the Salads and then brought it out to Madison. She was on the phone with the Diner putting in the order for lunch. It was going to be a long day for Alex as well as Max. She was going to be going over to help him move some of his stuff into her house. She has a shed that she can put some things into if there is not enough room in the house for his stuff so he can do what he wants to with it.

Max opened the door and walked in., I was just coming back to get you to take you to lunch. And Madison if she wants to come too?

We already ordered Salads for lunch. I did not know how long you would be.

Oh ok. I will go and get something then.

No, I got you one too. I always think of you. Bill had left to go to lunch already so it's just the three of us.

Ok thank you for looking out for me too Alex.

Anytime Max. I always try to think of everyone when I can.

I know you do. Are we still on for tonight after work?

Yes I will be over after work to help you load up stuff to bring over to our place.

Ok thanks. I am going to rent a truck this Saturday and I have a friend that is going to help me load up the heavy stuff to bring over. The table and chairs I am going to give to him since he is helping me and he needs them.

Ok Great.

Alex went back into her office and went over some emails.

We will know something next week about the trial.

Ok good. Is it for all three?

CJ has already pleaded guilty so he is already being sent to prison. So he will not be going to trial.

Oh good. Well that is one down. He will be going away for a long time then.

Yes he will. If the other two would just take the guilty plea it would be over.

Yeah but they are going to fight it. CJ knows he is guilty. No reason for him to go to trial. He took the deal.

Our lunch will be here shortly. So I need to get these applications put in order for today on who is coming in. I ran the background check for the one from yesterday and he is coming back in today too. I think he is one I am definitely going to hire on with the others. The others I will call back and let them know if they get the job. Then you can put them where you want them.

I called the Realtor today and I told her that we went for the loan yesterday and that we got approved. As long as we get in for the bid we are good. He said that he had someone else coming in to look at it too.

Yeah but they always say that so that you go ahead and put in an offer.

I am sure that no one else was going to come back and look at it. Not that day anyways.

After lunch the interviews started. Alex had gone through them all and all of them were on call back if they got the job. The one from yesterday was a definite hire but she would call him back tomorrow morning. She still had to go through the few that were for tomorrow before making her final decision. Only one was denied so far and that was from yesterday.

So how did the interviews go Alex?

I have five so far. I have a few more tomorrow. So once we get them in and see how they do it is to see how they work out. I think that we have to find out how well these people will work together as a team. I will keep those that want to work and get rid of those that do not want to work.

Ok good. Yes we always have to see who is going to actually work. I have seen some that actually want to work and do great work. Then some do not take their work seriously.

Hopefully these new hires will do well. They are going to be on a thirty day probation period.

That is why I put you in the hiring department. And you can fire them too if they do not work out. I got a call from Mr. Bryant. Once his place sells then he will put a deposit down on our building to buy it.

Oh good news.

Yes that way he does not have to get a loan to buy this he can just wait until he has the check for his place.

OK well I think that we are done here for the day. It's four in the afternoon. We should go and get the cars packed and bring stuff over to the house.

Sure we can do that.

Madison and Bill can leave now if they want.

Bill is already gone. He left an hour ago.

Oh ok I did not know that he had already left. Ok so Madison can go now too. We have to get busy on getting things done.

The rest of the stuff I will move over on Saturday.

Ok. That is fine.

Alex and Max got ready to leave. Madison was still working on something at her desk.

We are leaving and you can go too.

Ok I will once I get this done. I am just answering someone back.

Ok see you tomorrow. I have a few people coming in the morning, Madison.

Ok sure. Have a great night.

Max and Alex finished moving stuff into the house, there were just boxes of books and stuff that he did not need right now.

So let's go and get something to eat. We have to eat anyway. Or do you want to order pizza?

Oh yes, let's order a pizza. One pizza with everything?

Yes, that sounds really good. With extra cheese.

Oh yes you read my mind. We are going to be great roommates.

For sure. What about a movie?

Yeah we can watch a movie. Pick one out to watch.

Horror, Drama, Action or what.

Whatever you want to watch. You know how I am with Horror.

Ok Horror it is.

Oh you know how to get to me don't you Alex laughed.

I sure do. We will get groceries this weekend. Said Max.

Sure we can do that. Then we can figure out what we like to eat.

Max found a good scary movie. They both sat down and started watching it while waiting for the pizza to come.

Well that is part of the battle. I got all of the little boxes moved out of the way.

Yes, that is good. And they are in the corner of the room so you can get the big stuff in.

The doorbell rang. Oh that must be the pizza. Alex got up and answered the door and paid for the pizza. She put it on the counter and grabbed a few plates and put some pizza on them and brought them to the living room and handed one to Max. What do you want to drink?

I will take water thanks Alex.

Alex went to the refrigerator and got two waters out and went back to the living room and handed Max one. Then picked up her plate to eat her pizza.

This is great pizza. Where did you get it?

I ordered from the pizza place down the road. It's called Pizza Palace. They have great Italian food there.

Oh nice, we will have to order there more often.

Yes. I also order Chinese food too from another place close to here.

Wow. so when I do not want to cook I can just order and they will deliver.

Sure.

Ok so now I do not have to cook at all.I just order and have them cook it for me.

No it's not the same.

Oh did you see that? Max said.

Yes. And gross. That guy just killed that other guy by chopping his head off. Alex was just concentrating on her pizza and not the TV.

Yeah it was awesome.

Ok well not to me, said Alex. She could not watch any more until it changed. Well I am going to get some more pizza. Do you want more?

Oh yes I do. I do not turn down food. I will take two please.

Alex went out and got more pizza. Wait, why don't I just bring in the box. That way we can get what we want.

Ok, we can finish this tonight. No left overs.

Alex was glad that Max was moving in. Her lonely nights had ended. She loved working with him and going places together. She had wanted him to move in before when he had first said that he wanted to find another place to live. This was the perfect place for both of them.

After the movie Max knew that he had to get home and rest. The night was fun but he had to go home and get ready for bed. Ok I will see you in the morning.

Ok have a safe trip home.

I will. Thanks for dinner and the movie. It was fun. I always have fun with you. I will bring Coffee and breakfast in the morning.

Ok thank you.

After Max had left Alex cleaned up and went to bed. After the movie she had to watch something to erase her mind from what she had seen. She changed into her night clothes and climbed into her bed and turned on her TV. Max had his own TV as well to put up in his room so they both had a TV to watch in case they wanted to watch something else. She was satisfied with having him in the house. What happens can happen but until then she wanted to let things just go with the flow. She was not in a hurry to get with him because she was scared of something happening and ruining the relationship.

CHAPTER EIGHTEEN

Alex got to work and Max was already there. They were the only two in the building.

Hello Alex. Glad I got you before the others showed up. I have been doing a lot of thinking last night.

Alex's heart sank. He did not want to move in. She was crushed. What is it?

Well you had mentioned about getting a couple of kittens. And one of my friends has two that she found and she is not able to keep them. They are both females. I have a picture here for you to look at.

Oh sure, She breathed a sigh of relief.

Max pulled out his phone and showed her the picture. If we do not take them then she will have to take them to the shelter because she is not able to have them where she is.

Aw they are so cute. Yes, let's go and look at them later. Give her a call and tell her that we can take them. She will have to stop and pick up all the supplies that she will need later before they both go and look at them. She already knew that she was going to take them as Max is an animal lover. She loved cats as well. She had one when she was a child but when she moved out and went to college the cat died and it was too hard to get another animal right away. She was close to Scruffy as her cat was a persian.

Well we will leave early and get the stuff and go and pick them up. I will put them up in my room for a few days. So that way they can get used to the house. I really do not want them outside right now.

That will be a good idea. And I am not sure if you want to let them outside only because of the wildlife out there Max said.

Right yeah I think that it would be a good idea to not let them get used to being outside.

Anyways I have to get the interviews done so that we can go to lunch and then do other things before going to the store and then get the cats. I will pick up some toys and kitten chow.

Would you like me to stay the night, I can set up an area for them in my other room. Not in my bedroom but in my den and I can put the litter box and food in the closet there and just leave the door open. And then we can put the other litter box wherever you want to place them.

I can put it in the laundry room and then put the dishes in the kitchen so that they can eat there.

Ok now we have their potty places situated. I like the clumping litter because it is better for the cats.

Sure we can get that today. I think it would be much easier to clean. Anyways I have to see if my first interview is here. I have a few today and then I have to figure out who I am going to hire.

Ok I will be in my office. I hope that the Trial will go well next week. The families have been notified about it so that they can come to it if they want to. I told them that they did not have to be there but just wanted to let them know that they could come. I know for some people they really are not able to go into the courthouse during the trial. So someone goes and sits in for them.

Yes, that is ok for some people. I think that one of my interviewers is here. I hear Madison talking to someone. Alex got up to go out and talk to them.

When Alex walked out she saw two people sitting down waiting to be interviewed.

Hello who was supposed to be here first. A guy got up to go in to do the interview. Alex went into her office and shut the door. She had to get her applications on her desk

After the interviews were over only two were qualified for the jobs.

She walked into Max's office and asked if he wanted to go ahead and go for lunch and then after they could go ahead and stop and get everything for the kittens. Then they could work on the afternoon stuff that had to be done and then just leave and go get the kittens. We can just lock up and go if Madison and Bill want to go with us.

I really want to be just the two of us today.

Ok sure we can do that. They can actually close up and go themselves if they want.

Yes they can but today I just want it to be us. We need to talk.

Alex was not sure what that meant and she had hoped that he had not changed his mind about moving in. She had hoped that she had not made a mistake about him moving in. I think that it was in the best interest for the both of them. Her heart sank again. This was already tough and she overthinks everything as to be at its worst when it really might not be.

Where do you want to go?

What about the Italian restaurant?

Sure we can go there. It is close to the pet store where we can get the supplies for the kittens.

Ok good. Let's go. The three that I had interviewed, only two of them are qualified for the jobs. The other one did not have any training at all. But he did seem like that he would do well but I really do not have time to train anyone and he has not had the schooling either. So I will call them to come in next week to start. Hopefully Monday.

They both got into Max's car and went to the restaurant. When they pulled up the parking lot was half full. Well at least it is not busy yet. They both got out of the car and walked in the front door. The hostess came over and led them to a booth.

Is this ok? Asked the Hostess.

It's fine replied Max.

She handed them both a menu. Your waitress will be right over.

Thank you, replied Alex.

So we have to figure out what to name the kittens, said Max.

Well maybe we should see what their personalities are like. Sometimes that is a good way to find out.

Yes I agree, said Max. Max then opened up the menu and started to look at what was on the lunch menu. Oh they have Lasagna. That looks good. And I think I will get some Italian sausage to go with it.

Oh that does look good. But just then Alex saw the Stuffed shells. Oh I think I am going for the stuffed shells and the sausage also sounds good.

The waitress came over for their drink order and since they already knew what they wanted they also gave her their lunch order. Would you like a salad with that?

Sure I would like one with Italian dressing, replied Max.

I will have the same, said Alex.

Ok sure I will put that right in.

I had the spaghetti one time here and it was really good said Max.

Yeah I have eaten here before. I think I ordered food from work from here. I will have to remember that next time when I am at the office. Well maybe warehouse since we might be moving.

The waitress brought out the two drinks and the two salads and placed them on the table. Is there anything else I can get you?

Just some parmesan cheese for our food, replied Alex.

Sure I can do that. The waitress went back and brought out the parmesan cheese and placed it on the table. Food will be out soon.

Max and Alex started eating the Salad. Alex had wondered what Max was wanting to talk about.

How is your salad?

It's good. Thank you. How is yours.

Mine is good too.

So what did you want to talk about?

I was wondering if you wanted to make any changes outside of your place. Like maybe put in a hot tub?

Oh. Well I had thought about it once a while back but have not thought about it since.

I had a place with a hot tub and I loved it. And with the hours that we do I think it would be great to get one and place it out back behind the house.

Well we can go sometime to check them out. Maybe next weekend. Just to look at them.

That would be a great idea. We can get a price on them and go from there.

Yes I really want to save for one but now we have the warehouse to get paid for.

Yes that is true. But we still have to be able to relax at times. We can just cut back on going places.

Why don't we wait for a while to see what we want to do before making any kind of decision but I really like that idea. We could still go on a vacation though.

Sure we can. We deserve that every year. As long as Bill is there we can plan on a trip out of the area or even out of state.

Oh and maybe you can take a trip to South Korea. I mean I am here so you can go. I can handle things here.

And so can Bill. We can both go. You said something that you would like to go to one day.

Yes I would but not until we know that we have a good team going. I think that right now it is important for you to go and visit more than myself. You are from there and you need to go and visit family. I can go another time.

The waitress came out and brought them their food.

Oh this looks and smells great. Thank you.

Alex could not wait until she got into her Stuffed shells. These are amazing.

Yes it is. Here, try this lasagna. He feeds Alex a bite. What do you think.

Oh, it is really good. Maybe we should have gotten the sampler platter but I think that was listed in the night time meals. I can really taste the Italian seasonings in it.

We will have to stop some night and get that for our dinner.

After lunch they stopped at the pet store and got some things for the kittens.

We need a good clumping litter, kitten chow, dishes, litter pan, bed and toys.

Why get a bed. We already know that they will be sleeping with us.

Well I don't leave my bedroom door open. I have always slept with my door closed ever since I was young. I like my privacy.

So do I but since I will be upstairs I will leave my door open.

You know I was afraid you were going to change your mind about moving in.

Who? Me? Never. Alex, we are like Salt and Pepper. We get along really well and I like that. We work well together and doing things with you is wonderful. Thanks to you I have things to be able to do and not do it alone. I am happy that you plan things out to do. This is what I needed to have fun and relax.

Yes I am glad that you're doing these things with me. I have fun with you. While it was good to get away for myself but it is fun to get around with you too. To see your face on the new things that we have done was great.

Ok so what do you think about bowls for the kittens? Do you like these ceramic ones with the kitties on them.

Sure, They are cute.

Yeah I thought so too. Oh and I passed by some treats that I want to check out and we also need to get toys.

Yes we do need to get them toys. Some with catnip in them.

Yes I like those. I will have to put some of them in the living room for them to play with. I want to get a basket for them for their toys.

Ok sure. Are we ready to check out? I think we got everything, replied Max.

Yes, I think so. I have to get back to the office. I have to finish up stuff and call everyone and have them come in on Monday.

They made their way to the front to check out. Alex paid for the things for the kittens.

Back at the office Madison had a few more applications for her to go over.

Ok thank you Madison. Any other ones that come in just put them in an application folder. Right now I think that we have everyone that will work so far. I have five people so far and I want to work with them and get them in here so that they can see just what we do and also I want to see how they are going to work out.

Ok I can do that. I will just tell them that the positions are full. But you better go ahead and pull the ad so that they are not calling about the job or putting in the applications. I had one guy get mad because I had told him that the position had been filled. He said that he used to work undercover in Seattle.

Oh well I will definitely keep him in mind then. Where is his application at?

In your hand right now. It's the one on top.

Ok maybe I will call him in for an interview tomorrow.

Alex went into her office and called the person who used to work undercover. She had explained that yes they were full but she wanted him to come in for an interview and to join the team. She needed someone else that was good at what they do and since he had the experience she was excited to pull him in. After that she called all of the applicants that she approved of and told them to come in on Monday morning and that they would start working that day.

Max came in and told Alex that the Judge had called and said that the other two had come forward with a guilty plea so they would be going to prison as well so there was no need for a trial. But the media would be out waiting on the day that they get taken by the prison van to go to the prison. They knew that they did not have a chance so they decided to go ahead and get started on their prison time even though they were going to spend a long time there.

That is great news. So our case is closed. Now we can go ahead and finish everything up and then we can start getting everyone working on the cold cases.

Great idea. Ok so let's go and get the kittens. I want to stop by and get some clothes for tomorrow. I will stay at the house tonight to see how the kittens do. I want them to get used to me since I am going to be living there too.

Awesome so that way we can get them used to the house. You know what else we forgot. A pet carrier to put them in. We also need to make a vet appointment for them to get them in for their shots.

Ok sure. So we can get the carrier and get things set up before letting them come and investigate the house because it is going to take some time to get them used to the house. Then I will be there on Saturday to get them adjusted to the house more.

Well you can take tomorrow off to stay home with the kittens. We do not have much left to do.

Sure I can do that. Are you going to come here early or are you going to go home and get everything ready for Saturday?

Oh yeah. Why don't I call Madison and Bill and have them take the day off and that we will see them on Monday.

Best idea yet.

So I will run home and get some clothes for the house and then meet you at your house so that we can go and get the kittens.

I will go ahead and set up the house for the kittens then. That would be better to do it that way.

Yes I agree. That is a great idea. I don't know why I did not think of that before.Ok so I will drop you back off at the office so you can get the car and then I will run home and get a change of clothes, call Madison and Bill to tell them to take the day off unless if Bill wants to work tomorrow that will be fine. Then I will pick you up at the house and we will grab a pet carrier and go to the house to get the kittens.

Ok sure. I will see you then.

Alex had gotten home and she started placing all of the kittens' things around the house so that they could see that it was their home. To make it their home. She had placed a litter box up in the den upstairs as well as food dishes, Saturday she would have to put them in her bedroom while Max was moving in.

The door opened and Max walked in. He looked around and saw all the kitten things around. He was happy.

Hello. Everything here is Max approved.

Alex laughed and said well that is good. I am glad that you approve of where I had put everything.

Well, are you ready to go and get the kittens?

Yes I am, replied Alex. Did you call Madison and Bill?

Yes I did. But Bill still wants to come in and look over the other cases as well. He said that he might go in for a few hours.

Ok well that is good. Now that we will have extra eyes. Oh shoot. I still have one more interviewer tomorrow. I will go in for that time and interview him and then have him come in on Monday. I just want to meet him and see just what he knows.

Oh that is right. Well I will stay here until you get back tomorrow. Then I will go home and get everything ready to move here. Then on Sunday I will have to go back for a few hours and clean up everything.

Sure that will be fine. What about everything in the refrigerator?

It's already cleaned out.I do not buy a lot to put into it. I buy stuff for a few days because I do not eat at home a lot and when I do it is frozen stuff.

Alex and Max got into the car to go over and get the kittens. Even though they had just seen pictures of them, they both knew that they wanted them. They did not want them to end up in a shelter.

Max and Alex had gone and picked up the kittens and brought them back to the house. Max put down the carrier and opened the door. The kittens were not sure what to do so they stayed in the cage for a bit looking around at their new surroundings.

Alex grabbed some treats and placed them on the floor outside of the crate. One of the kittens decided to sniff the treat. Finally she decided that it was safe enough to come out and eat one.

Aww look one came out. She was an orange tabby with orange colored eyes. Well hello. How are you? The kitten grabbed the treat and then went back into the crate with her sister. Max was glad that the kitten was starting to feel a little safe as it came out of the crate.

Well let's give them some time to adjust. They just went from one home that they were feeling comfortable in and now they are in a new environment but it is their permanent home. Let's sit down on the couch and see what happens.

Max turned on the TV to find something to watch. Well let's watch a movie. Let them check out the house and go from there.

Well I will pick out the movie.I do not want to watch a horror movie and have nightmares later on. So what do you want for dinner tonight? I have pork chops in the fridge to cook up.

Sure that is fine. What do we have to eat with them?

I have scalloped potatoes I can make up. And what about some carrots?

Oh yes I love both of those.

Alex started dinner, she grabbed a bottle of wine and brought Max a glass.

Oh thank you, you're the best.

Here let me get up and help you.

No, you sit and relax. Maybe the kittens will come out and come to you.

Ok are you sure. I mean I can help, I don't mind. You do not have to do everything for me. I live here too so I can also cook.

It's ok. I can do this. It won't take long to do.

After dinner Max and Alex found a movie to watch. The kittens got out to investigate. They were starting to feel comfortable now and found the food dish in the kitchen and started eating. They both were getting hungry.

Well this is going to be a good movie. Do you want another glass of Wine?

Sure but let me get it.

Ok sure.

Max got up and grabbed both glasses and walked out to the kitchen. He noticed that both kittens were eating their dinner. Hey Alex come check this out.The kittens are out eating.

Alex got up quietly and went out to the kitchen. Aw look they are hungry. They are so cute. She got her glass of wine and decided to give them their space and went back into the living room to watch TV.

We do have to show them where their litter boxes are.

Yes, well I will make sure that they know where it is after they eat. That will probably be when they will want to go.

They both went back to sit down and watch the movie. Robin Williams really makes this movie a great one as he was a great actor. I love watching him in the movies. I am glad that we found this one.

After the movie finished they both looked for the kittens. They were both curled up on the floor together sleeping.

Look at them. They are so cute. Just sleeping there together. I am glad that we got them.

They will explore on their own time. Do you think that we should wake them up and show them where their litter box is? Asked Alex.

Let's let them sleep a little bit. I don't know how long they have been asleep. Poor things look so comfortable, replied Max.

But they have a bed and are sleeping on the floor.

Ok so what if we wake them. Show them where their bathroom area is and then bring them out to the livingroom to sleep?

Yes, let's go ahead and do that. And show them where their bed is at. But I really don't care where they sleep at night if they want to sleep with us. I guess I can leave my door open a little so that they can come in and out. As long as they do not play while I am trying to sleep.

Oh but they love to do that. And paw at your face and look at you as if to say, I want food NOW.

Well I am going to clean up the kitchen.

Thank you, dinner was great. I really like those potatoes that you made.

Thank you. They are from a box. But they are so good.

I will clean up the kitchen. Go and sit down.Max knew that Alex was tired and needed to rest.

Ok I will wake up the kittens and show them their litter box, you can show them where the one is upstairs. I set it up in the closet there and just left the door open. I think that we can also get a kitty condo for the living room so they can scratch on it.

Oh I forgot about getting one of those. Ok so go and do your things. I will clean the kitchen.

Thank you. Alex went and picked up both kittens and brought them to the laundry room.Once back on the floor they checked out their bathroom area, one decided to use it right away, the other one ran out of the room. Alex was glad to see one using it already. The kitten then ran out of the room and Alex followed. They both were found eating from their new dish.

Max had finished washing the dishes and was washing off the counters.

Wow you did a great job. Thank you so much.

Well of course. I do not do anything halfway.

So what do you want to do now?

Oh I don't know. Watch our little babies eat. I need to get them some wet food for them.

Yes, that is a great idea. But dry food most of the time. I would do canned food once a day.

Well let's go and sit down and see what they do. Alex grabbed her wine glass and filled it back up. Where is yours at Max.

I washed it already. I am fine. I grabbed some water.

Ok, Alex went over to the couch and sat down. So now what?

Well, let's find something on TV.

What about Law and Order? Is that on now?

I will check. Max flipped through the TV guide and found it and clicked on it to watch. I really love this show. I watch it all the time. Most of the criminal shows I watch. Which is why I love what I do.

Same for me as well. We watched it when I was growing up. It is what got me interested in what I do today. I have learned so much and just how much that it has affected them. The families I just can't get out of my head. I still think of them sometimes.

Yes I do too. Sometimes I have nightmares but I would not change it for anything. I feel more at ease when the person or persons are put behind bars.

I do too. Thankfully I do not have bad dreams about the victims. I just wish that it did not happen and that it was a bad dream. But then I know that it is really true. Those people who lost their lives were beautiful people. They did not deserve to die and it makes me work harder to find their killer. And for the most part we have found most of them. It's just sad to know that there are several cases that we were not able to get solved yet. But with the team we will be able to find out who did it.

I know we have failed those that we were not able to find their killers. They are out there somewhere. I think that they have left the area or are not from this area and that is why we have not been able to find them. I had read on the internet that one-third of the cases that are cold cases are from someone that is from another state or even from another country that was here for a short time and then some of them are hired to do the murder. More people will do it that way as there is less chance of them getting caught.

That makes sense.

Just then one of the kittens had found one of the toys and was walking proudly with it in her mouth. She walked over to her sleeping sister and dropped it on her head as if to say look what I got. Then she pranced her way out to the kitchen.

Alex and Max both laughed.

I forgot how cute kittens were, said Max.

Yes they really are. I never had two before. We only had one. But my friends had cats and dogs.

Max got up to see what the other kitten was doing and found her eating some more food. I wish we had gotten them some canned kitten food.

I do too but I wanted to make sure that they had the dry. Is she eating?

Yes. Glad she likes it.

Max went back in and sat down. They watched the news and then Alex decided it was time to go to bed. She left her door open a bit so that the kittens could come in if they wanted to sleep in her room.

Good night Alex. said Max.

Good night Max. Have a great night's sleep.

I will thank you. See you tomorrow.

See you then. Alex had turned on her TV in her room to watch before falling asleep. She was happy to have Max here tonight and the kittens. She figured that they would get into some kind of trouble during the night but she had hoped that they would settle down and sleep instead. They had plenty of toys and food and a nice little bed to sleep in. And they had each other. She was happy that she got both of them together.

CHAPTER NINETEEN

Max was already up and had made a pot of coffee, he was sitting in the living room watching TV. The kittens were curled up on the couch next to him sleeping.

Good morning, How did you sleep?

Well I slept great until a little someone came in and woke me up with her purring.

Oh no. Alex laughed. I think one slept with me last night. I found a toy on my bed this morning.

No, that was you. I saw you sleepwalk out to the living room and pick one up and squeaked it while you walked back into the bedroom. You want to see the video?

I did not, laughed Alex.

You did, I got it right here, he then laughed and said no you didn't. I just thought I would mess with you.

Alex went out and got a coffee cup and poured some coffee into it then went into the living room and sat down. So how long have you been up?

An hour, I think. The little rascals played for a while and then crashed. They are so good though. They use the litter box really well. I already scooped it up so it's clean.

Thank you, replied Alex. What would you like for breakfast?

Why don't you take a shower and I will make you breakfast. Eggs with cheese and some bacon to go with it.

That sounds wonderful Max. Thank you.

Alex got up and took her coffee with her, she got in the shower and got dressed. By the time that she was done Max had breakfast all done for the both of them.

Wow Max this looks good. Just like last time.

Well it's nice to cook for someone else besides myself. Enjoy. He also had poured her another cup of coffee.

Wow what did I do to deserve this?

Well if I didn't do it then you would and you have to go into work for a bit today. After you get done why don't we get lunch and then I will go home and finish up the rest of what is left to move over here tomorrow.

Sure that is fine Max. Do we want to go to the diner? I will call you when I am done and you can meet me at the diner.

Yes, that will be fine. Thank you. I will wash up the dishes while you're gone.

Wow, thank you so much. You know I did not have you move in to be my maid.

Oh I know. But there are two of us now and I can do my share around the house too. Thank you for letting me share your home. It's really quiet here at night.

You're welcome. I am glad to have you. She was really happy to have him there. He was a very handsome man and she felt safe with him. She knew that he would not hurt her. But she was sure that people would talk about her living with someone that she was not married to. So many people live together as roommates and do not have to get married. Although she was hoping that would be the next step, they would have to take it a day at a time.

After breakfast Alex had to leave to go to work for her interview. She would not be long so she could call Max when she got done. She just wanted to get the paperwork together before Monday so that would take a little bit of time.

When she got to work she found Bill in his office working on the case.

Hi Bill.

Hello Alex. Hey, look at this case. I think it is similar to an old one that was closed before. The same motive and the woman was killed almost exactly the same way. I think that we are able to close this one out soon. But I have to find out where this man is at and go and talk to him.

Great find Bill. Yes I think you might be right. This was the Miller murder. And it matches up to the Randall case. Well maybe on Monday you can take one of the new hires with you. But you get to pick out which one you want to take with you. Maybe the one that is coming in today. Keep your door open during the interview and let me know what you think about him. I think he is going to be a good fit.

Ok thank you Alex. I will. I am also going to go over a few other cases and see what I find in them too.

Ok, sure that will be great. So glad that Max had found you.

I am too. I enjoy doing this type of work. I have done it since I got out of high school. My Uncle used to do cold cases. Everyone else was busy with the other ones.

Just then the door opened up and a man walked in.

Hello. You must be Mr. Martin.

Yes, call me Jack.

Hello Jack. Come this way. They both walked back to Alex's office. Have a seat. So tell me about yourself.

Well I lived in Florida and I worked with my Uncle until he passed away last year. I moved here and I was working some with the police but I was bored. They really did not have much going there for me to work on. It was not their fault. They only had a few cases that I would work on. I need to be busy.

Well that is what I am looking for here. The police keep us busy that is why they do not handle as many cases as we usually get them. They are great as they help us out alot. My Partner and I stay busy and we have a few cases that we have not been able to solve yet and that is why we are getting a team together so that we can make sure that each case is solved. We handle a lot of cases here mostly murdered victims, some survive but they are not in good shape but they are recovering the best that they can and to have them go through what they have over and over again is hard. I think I am going to have you work with Bill on the cases that we have.

Sure I can do that. I work best at working the cold cases. I am determined to get them solved.

Thank you Jack. I am glad that I can count on you. I want you to meet Bill. He is working in his office.

They both got up and went over to Bill's office.

Bill, I want you to meet Jack. He had worked on Cold Case files and he will be working with you on the cases.

Hello Jack. How are you?

I am great. What are you working on?

It's a cold case that I have been looking at for a week now. I think I have it linked to another murder case. Would you like to stay and look it over?

Sure I will be glad to. Thanks.

Well I will leave you two alone. Thanks Bill.

Sure thing Alex. How are the kittens doing?

They are doing great. They are settling in.

That is good. Did you name them yet?

No but we will get them named soon. They have some great personalities. But we have just had them for a day so it will take time to name them.

Yeah that is great. Well good luck.

Thanks, I have to get the paperwork for Monday. Jack I will get you the paperwork to fill out over the weekend.

Alex went into her office and sorted the paperwork and gathered up for Jack and brought it over to him to take home. After she got all of the paperwork done she called Max to meet her for lunch.

At the diner Alex sat out in her car until Max got there. She sat out there for a few minutes before he drove up and parked next to her.

Alex got out and stood out front until Max got out of his car.

Hello. Did you hire the guy yet?

Yes I did. His name is Jack and he is working with Bill right now on the case.

That is awesome. I knew I could count on you. Did you get the paperwork done too?

Yes I got everything put together to hand out to the new employees. Hopefully they all show up now. But I think that they will.

I hope so too. Well, let's go and eat. I may even go ahead and move in some more things today. Is that ok?

Yes sure that is fine. I will put the kittens in my room while we get everything in.

Ok thanks. I will call you when I am on my way so you can catch the little critters.

Thank you, that will help a lot.

They sat down at a booth and waited for the waitress to come over.

The specials are on the board, said Alex.

I think I am going to have the fish dinner, replied Max. Fish on Friday is always good.

Yes it is. I am going to have the scallops. I see that they are on the list too. Lunch is on me today.

No, I am buying. You have been busy hiring new people to come in and help us. We need this. Thank you for all you do.

You're welcome. Thank you for all you do for me as well.

Not a problem. Hey I will save some of my fish for the kittens. They will love it.

Oh sure We can both give them some tonight. They are both going to be the most spoiled cats going.

Yes they are, replied Max. He was happy that they got the kittens. He did not want them to be sent to the Shelter that is a kill shelter and may not even make it out or even go together.

The waitress came over and got their order. She then left and came back with their drinks.

Scallops, fries and coleslaw. I love coleslaw. Alex loved her vegetables.

I do too. If it is made right. I also like kimchi. Have you ever tried it? Asked Max.

No I have not. What is it?

It is fermented cabbage. My mom makes it a lot and they have it almost everyday.

Oh well I will have to try it sometime.

The waitress came out with the food. It smelled so good.

After lunch Alex went back to the house and Max went back to the apartment to get things ready to bring over to the house.

Alex went into the house, the cats were nowhere to be found. She looked in the living room and they were not there. She went into the bedroom, they were not there either. She grabbed the treat bag and shook it and called them and they still did not come out.

She then went upstairs, they were laying on the bed that Max slept in last night, they were curled up together sound asleep. Max had neatly made up the bed. She would change the sheets when he got his room set up to sleep in. She did not want to change them if he was going to sleep up there. She quietly went back downstairs and put the fish in the refrigerator for the cats later. She did not want to wake them up. When Max calls and if they are still up there she will just go up and shut the door so that they do not get out while he is moving things upstairs.

She looked in the freezer to see what was there that she could make up for supper that night. She figured that Max would want to stay for dinner. Well she had hoped that he would.

She turned on the TV to watch the news. There was a problem at the jail. One of the inmates had gotten loose. She had to watch it to see what was going on. The reporter was out in front of the jail. Somehow one of the inmates had escaped. Seems to be with the help of someone inside. She had to see who it was and had hoped that it was not one of the men charged with the murders.

She called Max to have him turn on his TV. They both sat and watched. The person that the reporter had said that got away was CJ Brown. They could not believe that he was out of jail. How did this happen? And he was going to go to prison on Monday.

I think he knew that and he just wanted to see what he could get away with. Ok well I have to call Bill to go and watch Watson's house in case he decides to go there. Then he had to call the Watsons to let them know that he was out. Max will also call the police so that they could keep a watch for him in case he had gone there or sent someone else there. Just until CJ is picked up and put back in Jail.

So what I will do is drop off my stuff at the house and then go back to the office to see what else I can do like go out and look for him. I will keep you updated on what I find out.

Ok Max. Thank you. I hope that he is found tonight.

I do too but there are so many places that he could hide out at. I know that he has a lot of friends.

Well let me know if you get him.

I may have to go and unload tomorrow and then go and see if I can find him. I know that the police will be all over looking for him.

Check his house. I am sure that he will not go back there but there is always the chance. He may go back for something.

Max stopped by with the stuff and then was on his way out again.

If you want to come back here I can order food.

No, I think I am going to see what I can find as long as I can and if you don't mind I will stay with you tonight. Keep the doors locked and lock all the windows.

Do you think he will try to come after me?

He might. But I don't think that he will waste his time. I think that he will go after his kids and try to take them. Bill is there with another undercover police officer watching the house. The family should actually go to a hotel but I think that they are safer where they are now. Max left and went back to the office to look into where CJ would go. The only two places that he knew would be the childrens grandparents or his place.

Max had called Bill to find out if there was anything going on.

Nothing yet, replied Bill. But we are here for the night. I will call you if we see anything.

Thank you Bill.

Your welcome Max. The guy that Alex hired is really good. He is going to make a great part of the team.

That is great. I knew that I could count on her. Max left to go and see if there was anything going on at CJ's house. He locked up and drove over to the house. The lights were all off and nothing looked any different. He had decided to drive over to the grandparents house. He had to check to see if anything else was going on. He just had a feeling that they were planning something different, on foot. They know that they are going to be watched like before so they had to figure out another tactic. CJ will probably have some help to get into the house to get the children out and then drive off and out of state with them. Once they all go to bed that has to be when they will show up, so somewhere close by they will be watching the house.

Max called Bill to warn him. I believe that CJ is going to wait until everyone goes to bed in the house. Be on the lookout especially in the backyard. Something tells me that they are going to go through the back of the house.

We have the camera on it right now Max. Are you in the area?

Yes I am right down the road just in case.

OK. We could use some extra backup. If you see anything please let us know.

Will do. I am going to text Alex to let her know what is going on and to keep her informed.

Ok. Well I have to get back to watching the cameras. I think I see something.

Oh good. Let me know what it is. I hope that it is CJ. Are the lights off yet?

All the ones downstairs are. They are all upstairs now.

Ok good. Hopefully something happens soon then.

Well, look here. Bill saw CJ in the backyard. He is here. He is moving in towards the house and there is someone else with him. They are going to the garage, I wonder what they are getting.

Max texted Alex to let her know that CJ is at the grandparents house.

Alex looked at her phone and saw the text. She was so happy that he had been found.

I will tell you all about it later if you're going to be up. Max had texted her. So we should hopefully have him back in jail before morning along with his accomplice. Only the other person will not be going to prison. He will be going to jail for helping CJ.

Ok Max, I just saw the two get a ladder out of the garage and are taking it around back. Once we see them climbing up on the ladder we will go in and get them.

Thank you both for being out here. Now they can finally feel safe again once they are in jail.

Yes and CJ needs to be sent to prison soon. Whoever helped him get out of jail needs to do time too. Ok we have to be on the move.

Max got out of the car and moved towards the house. He could hear a commotion coming from the back of the house and the lights came on from upstairs again. The grandfather opened a window and looked out and saw CJ on the ladder. Bill had tackled the other guy that was helping CJ and CJ was made to come down the ladder. Max had gotten there just as CJ had climbed back down the ladder.

Well isn't this a surprise. What are you doing here CJ? Max asked.

I am here to take what is mine. My children.

Oh but you're not. See they are staying here with their grandparents because they are going to be the ones that are going to care for the children. Not you. You have already taken the main person that they love away from them. And you are going to pay for it. Now you have attempted kidnapping added to your sentence. I will make sure that you go away for a very long time. Max was angry that CJ had decided to do this to his own kids. How was he to support them without a job and on the run.

Bill loaded CJ into the van and took him and his partner to jail. Your brother is really dumb to think that you both would be able to get away and not get caught. Now he will do time in jail.

Max called Alex to let her know that he was on his way to Jail to bring in CJ and his brother Tom.

Oh so you caught him and his brother? Wow well that is good.

Yeah once they got the paperwork done he was going home to go to bed.

Ok see you tomorrow.

Thanks, how are the kittens?

They are good. They are laying beside me asleep.

Ok that is great. Well see you tomorrow. Max had hung up the phone.

Alex decided to go to bed. The kittens woke up as soon as she got up from the couch to go to bed. She went through and shut the light off and got ready to go to bed. She turned on the TV to see what was on and hoped that the kittens would settle down. She would have to get them situated in her room so that Max could move the rest of his stuff in by the afternoon.

CHAPTER TWENTY

Alex got up and fed the kittens. She cleaned their litter boxes and then she started her own breakfast. Today was the day that Max would be moving in. She was excited and nervous all together. It was nice to have him sleep at the house for the first time. Now he can get used to being here and comfortable. Alex did not want him to feel like it was her home but she wanted him to feel like it was both their home. Her phone rang and it was Max.

Hi Alex. We are loading up the rest of the stuff and we will be over to unload.

Ok sure. That is great. When you get here I will order food for all three of us.

That will be awesome, I am starving. We are almost done. Then tomorrow I will go back and clean the apartment. I will drop off the keys on Monday.

Sounds good. See you soon.

Alex went out to the kitchen to get a glass of wine. She would be helping Max move the things in. She would have to get the kittens into her room soon. She sipped on her wine and was very happy. Things were finally coming together. It will be nice to have someone to talk to everyday and to just cook for and be happy. She was falling for him even more now. He was very special to her. Just by the way that he looked out for her.

After an hour Max and his friend John showed up with the truck. They had backed it up to the porch. Max hopped out and opened up the back on the truck. They both got in and started to unload the boxes as the bigger stuff was in the back of the truck. Alex had the kittens in the bedroom and went outside to help.

After all of the smaller stuff was unloaded Max and John brought in the big stuff and brought it upstairs. They set up the bed and placed the couch and chair up in the other bedroom. When everything was done for the night Alex had ordered a large pizza and wings and had gotten out sodas for them. They ate dinner and watched a movie.

After Dinner Max took John home. He had to use Alex's car to take him home. Max would take the rental truck back on Monday. But he had to go and get his car from the rental place on Sunday.

Well this was a great day, Alex said after Max got back home.

Yes it was. I just have to go back to the apartment tomorrow. I just have to vacuum and then I am done.

Ok I can take you to pick up your car tomorrow.

Thanks, replied Max. Much appreciated.

Never a problem Max. You know that. I am happy to help.

So how was your day today? How are the kittens?

Oh, they are still in my room. I better go and let them out. They ate earlier so I will put a can of food down for them. Alex got up and went to her room. They were both sleeping on her bed. They woke up and stretched out and then jumped down on the floor and ran out of the room.

Wow look at them go said Max. I guess they are really hungry.

They are kittens. They are always hungry, Alex laughed. Kittens are like little garbage disposals. They eat everything so we have to be careful of what we leave around.

That is true. Puppies are the same but worse. They even eat clothes.

Yes they do. My friend's dog ate her socks.

Oh wow. So what do you want to do now?

We can just relax and watch TV. I am sure you want to relax after moving in everything.

Yes I am tired. I did not get much sleep after last night. That was intense.

I can imagine. What the heck was he thinking when he got out of jail and thought that he would not get caught again. We figured that he would try to go after the kids. He was determined that he was going to take them and leave. That is why he had his wife killed. So why attempt it again.

I guess that he wanted to make sure that it was not gone to waste. He did the first thing which was to kill his wife and then he would do anything to get to the kids even if it meant killing the grandparents. But he knew that he was on a limited time so he did not want to do that. Max was glad that it did not get to that.

I am just glad that he is behind bars again.

Yes and the person who helped him is fired and was also arrested.

Well that is good. If you're going to just let people back out and think that you're not going to get caught? How does that happen?

She put him in the laundry cart and rolled it outside for the laundry people to pick up. When she pushed it outside he slipped out of the cart and took off.

Well I am glad that he will be going away for a very long time.

Yes I am too. Someone like that is a dangerous person. It's just a bad mix. And if he had someone killed once he would do it again.

Do we want to watch another movie? Asked Max.

Yes, let's watch another one. Do you want some wine?

Yes please.

Ok two glasses of wine coming up.

The kittens were sleeping in a basket. They have a bed but they chose a basket to sleep in. Alex had to take a few pictures of them sleeping together. This is just too cute Max. Look at them. I guess they claimed the basket.

What do you keep in there anyways? Asked Max.

You know that would work great for their toys., But not if they continue to sleep in it. They are just so cute.

So pick out a movie to watch or whatever you want to watch.,

Ok Sure I can do that.

Alex brought over the wine and handed Max his glass. Here you go. Did you find anything yet?

No still looking. You know there are so many new shows out now. I do not usually watch much TV at home. I read a lot.

Reading is good. You can never get too much reading. It is probably better than watching TV. Do you watch the news?

That is one thing that I keep up on.I do watch the news. Only because with the way the world is today I have to keep up on that.

So have you heard from your family over in South Korea?

Yes and they are doing great. My cousin is going to have a baby.

Oh really. Wow. That's great.

Yeah it is their first one. I can't wait until they have it.

Oh that is amazing. Babies are so cute.

Yeah they are. Especially when they start getting older and they just get even cuter when they start to smile.

One day I hope to see that day. I have always wanted one.

Me too. Where can we get one?

Oh Max, Alex laughed. I don't know, plant a seed out back and water it and see what happens.

Do you mean that is how babies are made?

Yes, I think so. Alex was having fun and starting to feel more comfortable since Max had moved in. But she did not want to get too crazy and scare him off.

Hey, what about this show? These ladies are always on top of things. And their business is great. Who knew that decorating would be their speciality.

I used to watch them when I was a teenager. My parents liked to watch them, replied Alex.

Well we can watch this and then you can watch whatever you want. I am getting tired.

It's ok. Why don't you go ahead and go to bed and get some rest. We can get your TV hooked up tomorrow.

Sure that would be great. Ok well I will see you tomorrow.

Good night Max. Sweet dreams.

You too. Max went upstairs to go to bed. The cats had already woken up and followed him.

Traitor Alex said to the cats.

Don't worry I am sure that they will come down and sleep with you too, replied Max. He laughed a little.

Yes I am sure at like four am they will come down and stand on my face wanting food.

No they won't stand on your face, just on your chest batting you with their paw like your a toy.

You're enjoying this aren't you?

Why yes I am. Good night. Max went into his room and realized that he had to make up the bed. The cats jumped up on the bed. Max then turned and went into the guest bedroom. He still had to go through the boxes to find his bedding.

Alex decided to go to bed as well. Everyone had deserted her as it was. Of course who could resist Max. Definitely not the cats and for sure not her. She has been working her way in and he has noticed her and was happy.

CHAPTER TWENTY ONE

Alex woke up and layed still to listen for any movement up stairs. The cats haven't woken her up which was good. Must be they were still upstairs sleeping with Max. Now that he had the upstairs they could roam wherever they wanted. She got up, made a pot of coffee and then went in to take a shower. When she got done and went into the kitchen she could hear Max upstairs talking to the cats.

Max came downstairs, Well hello beautiful.

Alex looked around, Who me? Are you talking to me?

Yes you. And you are beautiful.

Oh stop you're going to make me blush.

Looks like I already did. Ok I am sorry. I will behave.

You're good but I am not used to all of this nice talk.

Why not? Guys do not talk to you like that?

No, not in a long time. I am too busy to even listen to stuff like that. Well except for you. I am never too busy to talk to you.

I am glad that you're not too busy for me.

Are you hungry? Do you want to eat now?

Sure we can go ahead and eat. I have to get the apartment done and when I get back we can go get some dinner and then I want to hook up my TV in my den and make my bed.

Ok and I have some clean towels in the bathroom up there for you.

Oh thank you. I will get a shower after breakfast.

Why don't you go ahead and get one now. I will make breakfast.

Ok well I am going to take my coffee up with me.

Sure. Is there anything special that you want to eat?

No, whatever you are making is fine.

Ok. I can do that.

Max had gone upstairs to take a shower.

Alex had breakfast all done when Max came back downstairs. She had made Scrambled eggs, sausage and toast.

Wow this smells so good.

Thank you Max. Enjoy.

Oh I will. This is so much better than living in the apartment. Great food, great roommate, great atmosphere and I just love it here.

I am happy to hear that.

I will clean up before we go. You made breakfast and I will clean up the kitchen.

Don't worry about the kitchen. You have to get your apartment cleaned. I will take you to get your car and I will come home and clean the kitchen.

Ok. But I will buy dinner later.

Ok I will let you do that.

Well it is not a debate. I am doing it anyway.

Ok. I give up, Alex laughed. You win.

After Breakfast Alex took Max back to get his car and then she went back home to clean. She turned on the TV to listen to the news and other news in the world, She then turned it over to the music station. She did some cleaning and started to wash clothes. She knew that she had to vacuum downstairs. She wanted to get as much done as she could so that she could relax for a while. The kittens were playing with a mouse. There were more mice around but they wanted to play with the same one. She took out a ball and rolled it across the floor, one of the kittens ran over to get it and play with it. What are we going to name you two? We will have to wait until Max gets back home to see what we are going to name you both. We can't just keep calling you kittens.

Max got back home a few hours later, well that is finally done. I brought home my vacuum, for the upstairs. I will take care of the upstairs so you do not have to come up at all, unless if you want to. So what have you been up to while I was gone?

I cleaned up the kitchen and am doing laundry. Replied Alex.

Oh Ok. Well let's go and get something to eat. I am hungry. Said Max.

Ok sure where ever you want to go and eat at. Asked Alex

Let's go somewhere we have not eaten yet? Replied Max

Sounds good, let's go. There is that place called Potato shack.

Oh yeah, let's try it. I love a good baked potato.

So do I. Especially if it is a loaded baked potato.

I like the twice baked potato. They are my favorite with sour cream. They are the best, said Max.

Oh yes they are good. I love my potato with sour cream. And cheese. Let's not forget the cheese. It is good with just about everything except for maybe Ice Cream

Well I am sure that there is a pregnant woman out there that can beg to differ.,

That is true.

They both got into the car to go to the Potato Shack. It was close to where they work, there are many restaurants near where they work which is why it is a great place to work. There is just so much to pick from.

They pulled in and the parking lot was full.

This is a pretty hopping place for spuds.

Yes it is indeed. Must be popular.

I guess so. Well this will be interesting. Maybe there is a potato bar.

Oh I never thought about that.

They both walked into the restaurant and they saw that it was full. They walked over to the sign that said please wait to be seated.

A hostess came over. How many.

Two said Alex.

Right this way. I have a cute little table for you in the corner by the window.

Oh nice, thank you.

They went and sat down, and the hostess gave them a menu.

Wow, look at what they have to offer. You get to choose any kind of potato to go with steak or seafood. Very nice menu.

Yes I agree, replied Max. It all sounds good. I think I am going to have the steak and shrimp with a potato but I want it twice baked with everything on it.

Oh yes that does sound good too. I think I am going to have the Scallops though instead of the steak with the twice baked potato.

The waitress came over to get their drink order. While she was there they gave her their order too.

Ok thank you. I will be right back with your drinks.

Thank you, said Alex.

So what do you think of the place?

It's really nice here. The farm tools on the walls are a great touch.

It really is. So did you have much to clean at your place?

Just had to clean the kitchen and the bathroom and then just vacuum, not bad.

That's good. At least now it is over. Now to get the upstairs put together.

Yeah I can work on it at night at least.

That is true. If you need any help with anything let me know.

Ok thanks.

The waitress came over with their drinks. Your order will be out soon.

Ok thank you.

So what do you want to do when we get home tonight?

I don't know. We still have not gone shopping yet.

Oh that is right. Ok we will do that after we eat.

Great. Thanks Max. I know you have things to do and I had totally forgotten to get groceries but I really do not know what else you like. I know some of it but not all of it. Like cereals and things like that.

That is ok. We can get them after. I have some things that I need to pick up.

The waitress came over with their food. Do you need anything else?

As long as we have sour cream and steak sauce we are good.

I will get you some sour cream. The steak sauce is on the table. So how many sour creams?

Two, said Alex.

Ok coming right up.

Oh this looks so good. Alex had picked up a scallop and ate it. She forgot to put butter on it though.

Mine is good too. The steak is cooked perfectly. I am glad that you said something about this place. It really is a nice, cute place.

Yes it is.

Ok here is your sour cream. How is everything?

It is really good. Thank you.

Great, let me know if you would like anything else.

Thank you, said Alex.

Ah sour cream to make the potato complete.

Yes for sure. Do you want to try a scallop?

Yeah sure I will take one.

Grab one. I don't want to pick one up for you. There is butter here to

Well thank you Alex. Max took his fork and got a scallop and dipped it into the butter. Thank you. I do like Scallops. Do you want some steak?

No thanks Max. You can have another scallop if you want.

Thanks Alex. I know what I am getting next time.

Or you can get a side order of scallops.

That is true. Yes I can get one and share it with you.

Well that is up to you. You may not want to share.

No, I will share. I would not sit here and eat all of these in front of you.

Are you sure?

Yeah I am sure. I am not like that. I like to share.

So do I. I think that is why I am glad that you decided to move in. You have the whole upstairs to hide in.

Hey I only have three rooms to hide in.

Actually four. You also can hide in the spare room.

Well I won't do that. Oh there is our waitress.

How is everything?

It is really good but can we get another order of scallops?

Just one?

Yes we are going to share it. They are really good.

Ok I will get that right in.

So now we can eat slower and have the scallops to go with our dinner too.

But I already have scallops.

That you do and you're going to have a few more.

Well thank you. I am so glad that we came here. We will have to come here more often.

Yes we will. Maybe we can come back next week after work.

That would be good. We are going to get fat if we keep going out. Now that I have someone else to cook for, I like it better to just eat at home.

Yes but you should not have to cook all the time.

I know. And I appreciate that.

Here you go, another order of scallops with butter. They are really good. I get them all the time.

We will be coming here more often, replied Max.

That is good to hear. Yes we have a lot of regulars here. On friday it is really busy with the fish dinners.

That is a great thing to know too.

At the store Max and Alex loaded up the cart with milk, eggs, cereal and meats as well as other things to go with the meat. What about fruit?

Yes, I like Fruit, Apples, bananas and oranges.

Ok so we will get those and I want to get some grapes.

What about chips and we need more wine.

Chips here yes wine no. I go to the liquor store to get the wine. If you want to get beer go ahead.

Ok I will be back. I will find you. Do you drink beer too?

Not really. Mainly just Wine.

Ok. See you in a bit.

Alex went down the chip aisle and picked up some plain chips. She wanted to get a dip to go with them. She also picked up some Fritos. She was going to make chili since it is starting to cool off at night. But then she would have to get cheese and sour cream to go with the chili as well. She already knew that Max liked her chili.

Ok I am back. Oh you got chips too.

Yes, I have to go back to the dairy department. I am going to make Chili this week.

Oh I love your chili.

Thank you. I learned it from my mom.

Well she was a great cook and you learned from the best.

I sure did. Thank you. My mom spent time teaching me how to cook and bake.She did not really have to work so she raised my sister and I.

She did great. With you anyways I don't know about your sister.

My sister turned out great too.

Which one is older?

She is. I am a few years younger.

That is nice.

Well let's get over to the dairy department to get what we need.

Back at home Alex and Max walked in the door and the kittens were quiet. They brought the groceries in the house.

They must be sleeping. Alex opened up a can of kitten food. Still nothing. Well they are sleeping somewhere.

There were toys all over the living room. Well they were out here playing but nowhere to be found.

Max went upstairs to see if they were up there. He found them on his bed. Alex, they are up here. Max had to wake them up. They followed him downstairs.

Here they come. Over here babies. Alex had put the dish on the floor. Both kittens came running.

Ok so what are we going to name these two. We have to think of a name.

Yes we do. Well one is orange and the other one is solid gray.

What about calling the gray one Smokey and the orange one Orange Juice?

What a great name. Orange Juice I like. Never heard of that one for a name.

Me either but I like it. Now we just have to get them used to their names. And I have to remember their names.

Its only two names Alex. I think that we can remember them.

Yes Max. I know.

Well let's get these groceries put away. Then I am going to go upstairs and set up my TV and get things unpacked.

Why don't I put the groceries away and you can go ahead and unpack.

I don't mind helping out. That way I know where things are.

Ok then you can go up and unpack.

Ok well I know where all of the cold stuff goes.

Thank you Max for your help but you really need to get settled in.

I am fine. I am getting settled in. I am learning where everything goes in the kitchen.

Well that is good. We will have it all put away soon anyways. It seems like a lot.

Most things go in the cabinet like canned goods and chips.

Bread goes in the bread box. Not the cat but the bread Max.

Oh now you tell me grinning at Alex.

You're going to get it, Alex lightly punched him on his arm.

I know. But I love picking on you. You're so much fun.

I know I am. But you're the only one that is allowed to pick on me.

Oh really.

Yes. I do not let anyone else pick on me. Only you.

Why me? Why am I special?

Because handsome, you are special.

Aww aren't you sweet.

Yes I am. Like honey.

Max gave Alex a hug. Ok now I am going to go up to my room and get to work. We will have to make a date to go out and go somewhere special.

We don't have to go to someplace special.

Yes we do. Because you're special.

Alex blushed. Do you want some help?

Well if you would like to come up and watch, come on. But I know where everything goes.

Ok sure. We can watch TV while I unpack.

Ok that sounds like fun. But I am also there to help.

They both go upstairs with the kittens behind them.

Well look who came up too. Guess now we will always have an audience.

No, I think that they just like being with us. For now. Wait until they get older.

Yes then they may want to be left alone. They are like teenagers then, they want to be with you as babies but as they grow older they are more independent.

Cats are more independent than dogs are. Cats have their own personality. While they need food to survive they can also hunt for food.

The kittens were checking out everything in the boxes as Max had opened them up as if to look for buried treasures. They chased each other around and then ran down the stairs.

Well I wonder what they are doing now. They are so much fun to watch them play together. I am glad that we got them. It has been awhile since I had a pet in the home.

Yes I am glad that we got them too. Otherwise they may not have gone together if they went to a shelter.

Max had unpacked everything in his room and broke down the boxes, took them downstairs to the recyclables. So what now. Are you tired?

Not really. Do you want to watch some more TV?

Sure we can do that. What about a comedy show?

Yes, That would be great.

Max turned on the TV and flipped through the channels to see what was on. He finally had come through one that he had not seen in awhile. MASH. What a great show.

My parents watched it when I was a kid. I loved it. I am glad to see that it is still running the reruns.

Yes, a great show. I watched it after we moved here. We get some of the shows in South Korea that are here in America.

You will have to tell me more about South Korea. Is it nice there?

It is very nice there. I miss it there and I miss my family but my parents wanted me to have a better life. But I feel that I would have had a better life there. I miss my cousins. We grew up together. Here I just have my parents, friends and you.

I am sorry that you feel this way. I can't imagine what that is like. I have my family here except for my parents but I can go and see them anytime. You have your parents here but your family is in Korea.

I have family in other countries too as well, not just Korea. I don't remember where they are all at but I hear from them once in a while. We keep in touch on Social media.

Well I am glad that you're here. I can't imagine working with anyone other than you. Or going on trips with anyone other than you. You're so much fun to be with.

Thank you and I love spending that time with you. Now we can spend more time with each other. It is definitely a blessing to be here with you.

Thank you Max. She leaned over and kissed him on the cheek. Well I have to get to bed. We have a long day tomorrow.

Yes we do. Good night.

Good night Max. Alex got up and walked to her bedroom and shut the door and got ready for bed. Once she was done changing clothes she opened her door a bit so that the kittens could come in if they wanted to.

CHAPTER TWENTY TWO

Alex was the first one up, she went out and made a pot of coffee. She then made her way back to her room so that she could get a shower. As she was getting ready she could hear movement outside the door. Orange paws batted around under the door. What are you doing Orange Juice? You can't come in here silly kitty. I have to get dressed. Another set of paws ran by. She could tell that Smokey was out there too. Then she heard a scuffle outside the door between the two and them running off chasing each other. She had to laugh. She then heard a crash. Alex ran out to see what happened.

The cats had run into the living room and knocked the books off of the coffee table.

What are you doing out here? Have you both been in the catnip?

Max came downstairs half asleep, What is going on?

The cats have gone crazy this morning. Alex picked up the books and placed them back on the coffee table and then went to the kitchen to fix a cup of coffee.

Ok well I am going back up to go back to bed.

What? Did you forget what today is?

Sunday right? Max laughed. I know I am going up to get a shower and get ready for work. Clothes are optional today, you know.

That is ok. I am going with clothes on. I suggest you do the same. I don't need all of the women in the area looking in the windows at you.

Ok if you say that I have to wear clothes then I will. That is why I made you a partner but I should have laid the rules down before I did so we could have this understanding.

No, the only place that clothes are optional are at home.

Oh really? Well where was my memo on that one.

Did you not read the fine print when you moved in?

No, I missed it. Ok I have to get ready.

Alex was now imagining him with no clothes on and she wanted to sneak a peek. She could bring up something and pass by the bathroom, she could tell he did not shut the bathroom door. Maybe that was an invitation to go up. She then heard Max yell.

Darn Cats get out of here. Leave my legs alone, I am not your scratching post Smokey.

Ah the attack of the kittens. Alex had to laugh. He also had parts that kittens did not need to be dangling from. And those parts had to be protected.

A few minutes later Max came downstairs with shorts on. He had to put some ointment on his battle wounds from the kitten shredders. Boy their nails are sharp. They tried to rip me to shreds up there. I am not their scratching post.

Alex had to hold it in and not laugh. Her face was starting to turn red from not laughing. Then she could no longer hold it in and let it all out. Once she got her composure and was able to stop laughing she apologized to Max.

Well it is funny but not as much when it is you that is being attacked by the killer claws. I am going upstairs to change now. I got to go and put on some pants to protect my legs.

The cats ran back upstairs after him. Cut it out guys. My legs are not trees for you to climb on.

Alex broke down laughing at that point.

Max yelled down to her, I hear you down there. Get a good laugh because the same thing will probably happen to you.

No, because I keep my door closed when I am in the bathroom.

Just wait. One day you will get yours. Max laughed. He put his pants on and shoes and then went downstairs to get a cup of coffee. He had already brushed his teeth when he got out of the shower.

Why don't we pick up breakfast on our way to the office?

Sure that will be good. We can pick up some donuts too because we have the new employees coming in today. We will see just who shows up.

When Max and Alex arrive, they had already dropped off the rental truck and Max rode with Alex to the office. They brought in a dozen donuts for everyone and Alex put them in the break room and made a pot of coffee. Now that there were going to be more people working she would have to get more coffee to keep the busy detectives going.

About nine in the morning everyone started to show up. Alex had them grab a donut and coffee or water and meet up in the conference room so that they could fill out their paperwork. She had seven new people including the one that came in on Friday. She handed everyone their paperwork and sat down to answer any questions if anyone had any. Once everyone had their paperwork done they were allowed to go and talk with Bill and Max. Alex took the paperwork into her office and looked everything over and then set it aside so that she can work on putting them on payroll for the week. Now that they are here and working they will all be put on salary and not on a time clock.

Bill met with everyone and talked to them about what he is working on now which is a cold case that he has. There are five others that need to be looked at to find out what they can figure out.

Max got a call from the judge. All three men were being taken to the prison in another county. Oh thank you for letting me know. That is great news. We can definitely close the case now. Max filled out the rest of the information on the paperwork and gave it to Madison to put into the computer and then file away.

Ok everyone it's lunch time. You can leave to go and get something to eat and then meet back here in an hour and a half.

Max and Alex went to the diner to eat, Madison stayed at the office and had her lunch there. Bill had left for lunch somewhere else with some of the guys.

At the diner it was busy, this is why they chose an hour and a half for lunch. They knew that they would not have enough time to eat and get back to work in an hour. The hostess came over and took them to their table. Handed them their menus and left.

The waitress came out and gave them a menu and took their drink order and left.

Oh look at the specials. They all look so good. I just don't know what I want to eat.

Me either. I guess maybe spaghetti and meatballs. That is what has my interest right now.

I think I am going to have the same, replied Alex.

Ok Great.

The waitress came over with their drinks. Ok, are you ready to order?

We sure are. Two spaghetti and meatball dinners please.

Ok sure thing. I will put that in right now.

Well this is good. The guys are on their way to prison right now.

Oh that is great news. They will be there for a while.

Yes they will. I am so glad that we were able to close this case and get everyone that was involved behind bars. Now the children can grow up and be able to move on.

So what do you think about the new detectives?

I think that we are going to work out fine. Everyone was here early and ready to go. All the paperwork is done and I have to go through and put all the information in for payroll.

That is good. I appreciate what you have done in the hiring phase.

Thank you Max. When we get back we can do orientation and go over what we expect from everyone. Bill will have a few people work with him and the others will do what is needed.

The waitress came over with their meals, they both ate so that they could get back to work.

What do you want to do for dinner tonight? Max asked.

What about a couple of subs.

Oh yes that sounds good. Turkey and swiss sub would be good for tonight. Then we can relax tonight.

Well you can. I still have another room to unpack.

Oh yeah that is true too. Well I can help if you need it.

I will be ok. I just got to get the book shelves moved to where they need to go and to put the books in them and other things that I have.

Ok well let's pay the check and go. I really don't want to go yet though. It's nice just sitting here talking with you.

Yeah but we will be doing that later anyways. Come on, let's go.

Ok, they went up and paid their bill and left to go back to work.

Have you heard anything more about the warehouse?

Not yet. So hopefully sometime this week we will be able to hear back from them.

Back at the office most everyone was back from lunch. Alex had everyone go back into the conference room to talk to everyone about the job and who would be doing what job. The others showed up a few minutes later. Alex was glad that everyone showed back up and was ready to go. Bill got the paperwork for the case that he had opened up to work on. Alex and Max had sat with them going over the case as well.

So who are the new employees Alex, Max asked.

Let's go into my office said Alex. I have the information in there. The guy that I had hired on Friday, his name is Jack. He started working with Bill that day. I am going to make name tags for them so that they can learn each other's names. I have Charles, Mike, Sammy, Nathan and Tommy. Those that have social media check out ok. I really think that I made the right decision on hiring these guys. They truly seem legit.

That is good Alex. Thank you. Now with this case closed we can focus on the cold cases until our next case comes up. I hope that we do not have another come up so we can get these cases done. With our team we can get through them easier with extra pairs of eyes. Max and Alex went back out to the conference room, Alex brought out tags and a marker. Passed each one a tag and had them write their names on their own.

Now that we know who is who, let's go ahead and start working on the first case. We have a map up on the wall. We will put a pin in the map for where each murder was taken place. Now we need to find out the persons responsible for each case. There are five all together.

By the end of the day Max and Alex were ready to go home and relax. They wanted to be able to entertain the kittens or have the kittens entertain them. They stopped by and picked up some subs for them for dinner and went home.

Well I wonder where the kittens are now.

I don't know just don't go in with shorts on just yet.

I know. This is going to be tough when it's hot out again.

For sure. Neither one of us will be able to wear shorts for awhile. Little stinkers. I will have to trim their nails tonight. Well let's eat.

After dinner Max and Alex curled up on the couch with the kittens to watch a good movie. The kittens both fell asleep next to each other on the couch. Max and Alex had their wine and teased each other.

Great job today Alex. You really did well.

Thank you Max. I am glad that everything worked out.

Yes I did too. Would you like some ice cream?

Sure thank you.

Max got up and dished up the ice cream and handed one to Alex and then sat down on the couch. The kittens woke up just in time to check out what they were eating.

Oh look, they want some now. Alex got up and went out to the kitchen and put some ice cream into a small bowl. It was vanilla so it would not hurt them. The kittens started eating it after they were done sniffing it.

Well I am going to go to bed, said Alex.

Yeah me too. I want to watch the news. Good night Alex.

Good night Max.